GULLAH FOLKTALES
FROM THE GEORGIA COAST

GULLAH FOLKTALES
FROM THE
GEORGIA COAST

Charles Colcock Jones Jr.

Foreword by Susan Millar Williams

BROWN THRASHER BOOKS
The University of Georgia Press
Athens & London

In memory of Monte Video Plantation, and of the family servants whose fidelity and affection contributed so materially to its comfort and happiness.

Published in 2000 as a Brown Thrasher Book
by the University of Georgia Press
Athens, Georgia 30602
Foreword by Susan Millar Williams
© 2000 by the University of Georgia Press
All rights reserved

Printed and bound by Creasey Printing Services

The paper in this book meets the guidelines for permanence
and durability of the Committee on Production Guidelines for
Book Longevity of the Council on Library Resources.

Printed in Canada
00 01 02 03 04 P 5 4 3 2 1

Library of Congress Cataloging-in-Publication Data

Jones, Charles Colcock, 1831–1893.
Gullah folktales from the Georgia coast / Charles Colcock Jones ;
foreword by Susan Millar Williams.
p. cm.
Originally published: Negro myths from the Georgia coast
told in the vernacular. Boston : Houghton-Mifflin, 1888.
With new foreword.
"Brown Thrasher Books."
Includes bibliographical references.
ISBN 0-8203-2216-4 (pbk. : alk. paper)
1. Gullah—Georgia—Folklore.
2. Tales—Georgia—Atlantic Coast. 3. Animals—Folklore.
I. Jones, Charles Colcock. II. Title
GR111.A47 J69 2000

398.2'089'960758—dc21   99-089728

British Library Cataloging-in-Publication Data available

Originally published in 1888 as
Negro Myths from the Georgia Coast
by Houghton-Mifflin, Boston

PREFATORY NOTE

Mr. Joel Chandler Harris has, in an admirable way, commended to public notice the dialect and folk-lore in vogue among the Negroes of Middle Georgia. With fidelity and cleverness has he perpetuated the legends and songs once current among these peoples, and now fast lapsing into oblivion. There is, however, a field, largely untrodden, in which may be found ample opportunity for the exhibition of kindred inquiry and humor. We refer to the swamp region of Georgia and the Carolinas, where the lingo of the rice-field and the sea-island negroes is *sui generis*, and where myths and fanciful stories, often repeated before the war, and now seldom heard save during the gayer moods of the old plantation darkies, materially differ from those narrated by the sable dwellers in the interior.

In confirmation of this suggestion we record the following Negro Myths from the Georgia Coast.

Augusta, Georgia, March, 1888

CONTENTS

FOREWORD

SUSAN MILLAR WILLIAMS

When Charles Colcock Jones Jr. learned to talk, his first word was *gone*. It was a word that would become a refrain during his long, productive life and the unifying theme in his fourteen books, more than sixty shorter works, and thousands of letters. A sense of loss pervades Jones's prodigious literary efforts, and *Negro Myths of the Georgia Coast* (retitled in this edition as *Gullah Folktales from the Georgia Coast*), one of the earliest and most enigmatic collections of coastal African American folklore, exists because near the end of his life Jones was worried that such tales were about to vanish along with the plantations and slaves of his youth and the mound-building Indians who came before them. And he was right. For although scholars continue to discover modern variants of these tales, the versions Jones transcribed in the 1880s are now regarded as a kind of window through which we can peer backward to the oral traditions of an even earlier time.

The glass in that window, like all old glass, is bubbled and distorted. The questions a modern folklorist yearns to ask are mostly unanswerable—who were the informants, how were they interviewed, how old were they? Which stories were told by men and which by women? Where did the storytellers live at the time of the interview and where did they grow up? How accurate were Jones's transcriptions? And, perhaps most interesting of all, did the tellers alter the traditional tales to tell Jones what they thought he wanted to hear?

Unfortunately, no one knows. Only five informants are identified by first name—Jupiter, Smart, July, Cudjoe, and Sandy—all prefaced with the title *Daddy*, an honorific used by both blacks and whites to express respect when addressing elderly black men. No surnames are given. Jones dedicates the volume to the memory of Monte Video Plantation and the faithful family "servants," a term the Joneses had always preferred (even before the Civil War) to the blunter "slaves." Contemporary folklorists assume that Jones went back to one or more of his family's plantations, Montevideo, Arcadia, or Maybank, in the old ricegrowing regions south of Savannah, Georgia, and sought out the oldest residents, who told stories as he took notes. Yet we have no positive proof. Jones might have collected these tales from several localities. He may have reconstructed them from childhood memories, embellished them, or even made them up. The simple fact that Jones was a white man trading in African American narratives is enough to raise suspicions about both his motives and his methods. Yet his personal history made him one of the *only* people both qualified and motivated to compile such a collection in the 1880s.

Jones was born in 1831 in Savannah, Georgia, a city he would later serve as mayor. His family owned over a hundred slaves who cultivated rice and sea island cotton along the Newport River in Liberty County. The Joneses seem to have had no qualms about owning slaves. Charles's father, Dr. Charles Colcock Jones Sr., was a Presbyterian minister so obsessed with the health of slaves' souls that he came to be known as the "Apostle to the Blacks." In fact, Reverend Jones was on the road proselytizing during most of Charles's childhood (the source of that early fixation on the word *gone*, according to his biographer, James Berry) and the family's life was organized around the spiritual labors of the great man. The elder Jones spent much of his life elaborating a creed that attempted to reconcile his role as a minister of the gospel with the need to make a profit on his plantations. "Thou shalt love thy neighbor as thyself," the elder Jones admonished fellow slaveholders, "and who are our neighbors if the Negroes are not?" The Bible sanctioned slavery, but in doing so it imposed duties on masters as well as servants. Masters should take good care of their slaves, paying careful attention to their health and comfort and spiritual instruction in part because, as he bluntly put it, "virtue is more profitable than vice." Healthy, happy, Christian slaves were more likely to "advance" the "pecuniary interests of masters."[1]

As a child Charles Jr. seemed likely to follow in his father's footsteps and become a preacher-planter. By the time he went off to South Carolina College it was apparent that he had other interests, among them a passion for Indian relics that would eventually grow into a scholarly obsession with the southeastern mound-building tribes. (He would become the first president of the American Anthropological Association, and his collection of Native American relics was one of the largest in the world.) When young Charles went north to Princeton and then to Harvard Law School, his letters home were filled with requests not only for more money but also for alligator skeletons and arrowheads. A neighbor with whom his parents shared these letters gossiped that they reeked of tobacco, concluding that Charles, out from under his father's thumb, had taken to smoking and chewing. (All of the Joneses were prodigious letter writers; their correspondence from 1854 through the late 1860s was published by Robert Manson Myers in 1972 as *The Children of Pride.*)[2]

Well before the outbreak of the Civil War, the Joneses were seriously discussing whether it was wise for the younger generation to continue planting. Charles's younger brother Joseph was studying medicine; his sister Mary was being courted by an earnest young minister. Their father, aware that the world was changing, advised young Charles that the life of a planter required a full-time commitment and so did the life of a lawyer. After much discussion, Charles decided to sell most of his slaves and use the money to further his education and set up a law practice. Though he took considerable pains to ensure that families would not be separated and that every person would go to a kind master, this sale eroded some of the family's most cherished principles, exposing the fact that slaves were not part of the family but were instead negotiable property. Jones was indignant when he later discovered that his stipulations had been ignored by his broker, but by then, of course, the deed had been done, and control was lost. He and his father exchanged a series of anxious letters assuring each other that the sale was necessary and that they had only had good intentions.

Jones took up the practice of law in Savannah, and, in fine aristocratic style, without the indignity of campaigning, was elected first alderman and then mayor of the city. He married his cousin Ruth and the two had a baby girl. In 1861, at the age of thirty, Charles seemed destined for a life of security, prosperity, and respect. And then, just as the South seceded from the Union, a cloud of bad luck came to hover over his happy little family. First, the baby died of scarlet fever in July 1861. Then, after safely delivering their second daughter a few days later, his wife Ruth succumbed to puerperal fever.

When Jones joined the Confederate Army to serve with an artillery regiment, this frail and sickly infant had to be left behind in the care of his mother and father. While Jones was away fighting in the war, Charles Sr. sickened and died. When Savannah and then the rest of the South fell to the Yankees, Sherman's army marched through Liberty County, burning one of the Jones family homes and pillaging the others. To the surprise of both Charles and his mother, most of the "servants" immediately defected, especially the field hands, and those who stayed demanded higher wages than the Joneses felt they were worth. Charles privately called them "wretched ingrates" and resolved to sell the land. But the market was flooded with ruined plantations, and he could not find a buyer. He worried about his widowed mother, who was left trying to impose her will on indifferent laborers through a recalcitrant overseer. However, Charles, who had remarried after Ruth's death, did not offer to move back to the plantations or even to nearby Savannah. Instead, determined to make some money and to rise from the ashes of war, he and his new wife Eva reclaimed his daughter from his mother's care and moved north, to New York City. There he found plenty of work for a lawyer, both paid and *pro bono*, and when he could he sent money home to help his mother with expenses. For several years he made it his business to press the claims of dispossessed plantation owners trying to reclaim their lands.

It was during this self-imposed exile in enemy territory that Jones became a historian and man of letters. Soon after the war, he, his mother, his sister Mary, and his brother Joseph scraped together enough money to print the first volume of his father's pet project, *A History of the Church of God During the Period of Revelation*, a huge tome that had consumed the family's energies for most of Charles's life. Joseph sent the unexamined manuscript off to be typeset, and the proofs were then forwarded to Charles for correction. Charles was appalled to discover that they had paid to print a *very* rough draft; whole sections were little more than scattered musings, and sometimes Charles Sr. had not cast his thoughts as complete sentences. Though the dutiful son admitted his disillusionment only to his mother and two siblings, and then only in careful language that attempted to spare his mother's feelings, it is clear from his letters that Charles was dismayed at his father's sloppy scholarship. (The family was inclined to put most of the blame on a man Reverend Jones had hired before the war to make a clean copy. In addition to botching the manuscript, they claimed, he had impregnated one of the family servants!)

Charles set to work filling the book's gaps and checking facts, and after months of late-night labor he was satisfied that the text was fit to publish. The first volume met with profound indifference from a cash-less southern public, and he convinced his indignant mother that there was really no point in going on to print the second one. Having discharged his filial duty to his own satisfaction, if not to his mother's, he moved on to write about matters closer to his heart. He began with firsthand accounts of the Civil War, including the Siege of Savannah. Eventually, he branched out to other areas of Georgia history, pushing backward to the Colonial period and the Revolutionary War. Jones moved home to Georgia in 1877; instead of settling near the coastal landscape of his childhood he chose the city of Augusta, near the mountains. He brought with him a mind honed and broadened by contact with the outside, though his nostalgia for the Old South intensified.

Much of Jones's energy now went into memorializing the Lost Cause. He was infuriated by fellow Georgian Henry Grady's famous "New South" speech, delivered in New York City in December 1886, which argued that the South of slavery and secession was dead, to be replaced by a South of union and freedom driven by commerce and industry. Jones bitterly opposed the New South movement, which proposed drowning out the wails of mourning with "the whir

xviii

of the spindle, the buzz of the saw, the roar of the furnace and the throb of the locomotive," as his arch-enemy Richard H. Edmonds put it. With his flowing white locks, "mellifluous" voice, and reactionary annual speeches to the Confederate Survivors Association, Jones was regarded by the younger generation as not just quaint, old-fashioned, or foolish but, as C. Vann Woodward succinctly observed, almost a "mummy."[3]

Yet speechifying and his Colonel Sanders suits aside, Jones was anything but a mummy. He was more like an ancient Egyptian embalmer, a skilled technician whose mission is, simply, to preserve. Always curious, always thinking, always describing and cataloging the world around him, he saw it as his duty to construct a record of the people and ways of life that were passing as well as those that had already passed into obscurity.

Gullah Folktales from the Georgia Coast is a collection of folktales in the Gullah dialect of coastal Georgia, and it is something of an anomaly in Jones's literary career. Its publication in 1888 pushed him into the center of a rancorous debate that dates to the beginnings of the American folklore movement and has its roots in our national obsession with race and status. The very concept of "folklore" was new in 1888 and was still being defined. In fact, the first issue of the *Journal of American Folklore* came out in the same year *Gullah Folktales* was published.

Experts agreed that "the folk" could be character-
ized as "backward peoples," members of isolated,
illiterate societies with strong oral traditions. In
Britain, they were the subsistence farmers who popu-
lated remote villages. The Romantic Movement had
created a vogue for these "noble savages," simple and
close to nature; at a time when the dark, satanic mills
of industrialization were ubiquitous, there was a wave
of nostalgia for pastoral life. The American scholar
Francis James Child published the first volume of his
five-volume set, *English and Scottish Popular Ballads*,
in 1882, causing a sensation on both sides of the
Atlantic. Suddenly, Americans started looking around
for a folk tradition of their own.

There was plenty to discover, north, south, east, and
west. In America, however, the search for "backward
peoples" ran smack into the question of race. The
pursuit of native ballads led naturally to Negro
spirituals, some of which had already appeared in
national magazines. Thomas Wentworth Higginson
(an abolitionist, the organizer and commander of the
first regiment of black troops during the Civil War,
and Emily Dickinson's mentor), published an essay on
spirituals in the *Atlantic Monthly* in 1867, and in the
same year W. F. Allen produced a book entitled *Slave
Songs of the United States*. The vogue for African
American songs eventually led the public to an inter-
est in black folktales, which were described in such

articles as "Folk-Lore of the Southern Negroes," published in *Lippincott's Magazine* in December 1877.

While academics and serious journalists were beginning to take notice of distinctly African American forms, these songs and stories were simultaneously being absorbed into mainstream entertainment. Among the magazine-, book-, and newspaper-buying public, which in that day was mostly white, there was a craze for humorous tales written in dialect. Almost any dialect would do, but black dialects were especially popular. Feeding this appetite was a host of nameless hacks paid to fill newspaper column space with minstrel-show type jokes. The taste for quirky regional speech patterns was also satisfied by "local color" writers like Charles Waddell Chesnutt and George Washington Cable, who used dialect as a literary device to highlight the quaintness of their characters. At the top of the heap stood Mark Twain, a literary genius whose instinct for the patterns of human speech raised the use of dialect to the level of art.

The star of the show was Uncle Remus, the creation of Jones's fellow Georgian Joel Chandler Harris, a white newspaperman who skyrocketed to fame and fortune by repackaging African American folktales as bedtime stories for children. Harris's Uncle Remus tales first appeared without fanfare in the *Atlanta Constitution* in the 1870s in a column he took over from another dialect writer, "Si" Small. The book *Uncle Remus: His Songs and Sayings* was published in 1880, and soon afterward Uncle Remus became a household name both in the United States and abroad. Rudyard Kipling, whose work would also become wildly popular, remembered that in his English boarding school groups of boys memorized Uncle Remus tales word for word and shouted them out in unison.[4]

Moreover, Uncle Remus's fame has lasted. I suspect that almost everyone over forty who grew up in the United States has heard of him, if only because of the Disney movie *Song of the South*. It is almost impossible to read Jones's tales without wondering about his relationship to Harris, since these stories too are about the exploits of Brer Rabbit, Brer Wolf, and Brer Fox. The connection, as it turns out, is not at all obscure. Jones started collecting African American folktales because Joel Chandler Harris asked him to.

Originally, Harris seems to have thought of himself as a good amateur scholar—a pioneer folklorist, linguist, and anthropologist. Yet almost before *Uncle Remus: His Songs and Sayings* had rolled off the press, he found himself under fire from professionals, demanding proof that the tales were authentic and that variants existed in other places. Meanwhile, Harris's publishers were demanding more storybooks and he was running out of material. Harris wrote Jones—who by then was well-known as a historian—in March 1883 when Harris was working on a sequel called *Nights with Uncle Remus* to ask if Jones knew of anyone who could tell similar stories. Harris mentioned that a woman in Darien, Georgia, had sent him several tales from the coast.[5]

Jones took Harris's idea and ran with it. Over the next five years he transcribed fifty-seven tales in Gullah dialect, to which he added four essays in his own patrician voice. Many are familiar stories—Brer Rabbit and the Tar Baby (*Buh* Rabbit in Jones's version), Brer Rabbit and the butter, the tortoise and the hare. But for anyone raised on the Remus versions or Aesop's fables, these pages will seem strange, exotic, off-kilter, like hearing Jack and Jill recited in Yorkshire dialect, where a hill is a fell and a pail is a piggin.

Many of the differences between the Jones and Harris versions can probably be attributed to geography. Harris was from the town of Eatonton in central Georgia, where the local black dialect would have been more-or-less intelligible to other Americans. Jones's stories, on the other hand, came from what Fanny Kemble once called the "savage selvage of civilization," the deepest pockets of Africa in America, where the language was a mystifying mix of English and several West African tongues. For the uninitiated reader, *Gullah Folktales* may seem at first glance to be virtually incomprehensible.

But if deciphering an unfamiliar language is the

biggest challenge one must meet in order to read *Gullah Folktales*, it is also one of the greatest pleasures. Familiar words and phrases metamorphose into a kind of poetic strangeness. In "Buh Rabbit an Buh Wolf Funeral," for example, after Wolf pretends to be dead and tricks everyone into coming to his funeral, the people are outraged at being played for fools and "bemean" him until he is ashamed to show himself for many days. What a wonderful connotative word, *bemean*—fashioned, no doubt, from *bemoan*, *demean*, and *berate*, with a fully-intended emphasis on *mean*!

Jones's version of the familiar Tar Baby tale illustrates many of the distinguishing characteristics of Gullah. "Buh Wolf and Buh Rabbit, dem bin lib nabur," the story begins. [Brother Wolf and Brother Rabbit were neighbors.] "De dry drout come. Ebry ting stew up. Water scace. Buh Wolf dig one spring fuh him fuh git water. Buh Rabbit, him too lazy an too scheemy fuh wuk fuh isself. Eh pen pon lib off tarruh people." Jones captures the sing-song rhythm of Gullah—"Eh pen pon lib off tarruh people"—the repetitions—"dry drout"—and the phrasings that strike our ears as odd, even backward, yet also exactly right: when the drought strikes, "Ebry ting stew up." As the story unfolds, there are other oddities. *V*s and *w*s are transposed, *t* is substituted for *th* in words like *thing* and *thief*, and there is no *s* on possessive nouns. *Other* is pronounced *tarruh*. *Scarce* is pronounced *scace*. "Buh

xxiv

Wolf, Buh Rabbit, an de Tar Baby" may be difficult to read, but it is a strong story, and eventually, with the help of Jones's glossary, it yields its secrets.

One recent book, Harold Courlander's *Treasury of Afro-American Folklore*, published in 1996, reproduces many of Jones's tales translated into standard English on the ground that Jones, like many of his peers, was interested in dialect for all the wrong reasons—because it sounded strange, because it evoked a white nostalgia for slavery, because it could be used to suggest that blacks were unable to speak standard English. Yet in the same book Courlander presents other unaltered excerpts from *Gullah Folktales* as faithful transcriptions of the Gullah language.[6] Such inconsistencies inevitably lead one back to the most troubling questions about Charles Colcock Jones's motives and how they may have affected his scholarship. How seriously can we take these tales as artifacts of African American history? Are they tainted? If we reject them on this basis, what texts do we have left to take their place as a record of African American oral traditions as they evolved during the stormy second half of the nineteenth century?

It is clear that both Harris and Jones saw themselves as preservationists and regarded the tales they brought into print as relics of a vanishing world. There was a good deal of talk in their day about the "scientific" value of African American folktales, a concept that would have appealed to the intellectual in Jones. But for him, even more than for Joel Chandler Harris, the tales were more than museum pieces or curiosities. They were emotional touchstones, wafting him back to the sights and sounds, the joys and terrors of his childhood. In writing them down, he was undeniably acting within a postwar tradition described by John Szwed and Roger Abrahams as peculiar to former slaveholders and their children—their affection, even reverence, for the speech patterns and folk beliefs of the "old types" that had at its root the Old South argument that superstition and ignorance made blacks incapable of surviving without white paternalism.[7] One of the charges perennially leveled at the Remus books is that Harris paints a sentimental picture of happy darkies and benevolent whites while the tales themselves are allegories of conflict between the oppressed and the oppressors. Charles Jones believed that slavery was a benevolent institution, but he did not invent a fictional character to serve as his mouthpiece.

The most remarkable thing about *Gullah Folktales* is Jones's willingness to let African Americans tell their own stories. He provides only the barest of introductions, one page, that explains that the tales come from coastal Georgia and are variants of those collected by Harris in the interior of the state. Then he simply gets on with the stories, where lions, tigers, elephants, and monkeys rub shoulders with creatures of the Georgia coast—porpoises, marsh hens, king crabs, and gallinippers (pileated woodpeckers), sharks, sea turtles, and sandflies. The main characters are pretty much the same forest animals as in the Uncle Remus stories, Buh Rabbit, Buh Fox, Buh Wolf (who here takes over from Buh Fox as Buh Rabbit's nemesis), Buh Bear, and Buh Partridge, along with possums, raccoons, fowl-hawks, owls, jaybirds, and eagles. The familiar tale "The Tortoise and the Hare" appears here as "How Buh Cooter Fool Buh Deer."

Jones does not limit himself to tales about talking animals. Several stories depict whites and blacks interacting, usually in a way that emphasizes their inequality but makes the point that each ultimately gets what he wants. In "De Ole Man an de Coon," for example, a rich white man has a wise old servant who came from Africa and is said to know everything about everything. The white man brags to his friends about his servant and takes bets that he can answer any question. So the whites send a boy out to catch a raccoon and seal it in a barrel. Then they send for the "ole Afreka nigger," show him the barrel, and ask him what is inside. He has no idea and says, "Mossa, hoona done head de ole coon dis time." What he means is "Master, you've outwitted me this time," but the white men hear the reference to "having the old coon" and think he has supernatural powers. They give the old man "big praise," and the master wins the bet.

He shares the money with the old man, and everybody is happy.

The story confirms one of Jones's most cherished ideas, that slavery is good for everybody. But seen from the original storyteller's point of view, the narrative has a different message. When black people say that the old man knows everything, they mean that he is wise in the ways of the world. The white man, on the other hand, sees a black man who "knows everything" as a carnival magician who can be exploited as a curiosity and who can bring in extra cash.

In "De Ole Man an Det," the trick is on the black man. An old man gets tired of working, but white people keep giving him tasks. He takes to praying, loudly and in public, that Death will come and take away the master, the mistress, and the overseer. The whites decide to frighten him so he will never do it again. The master dresses in a long white robe and goes to the old man's house. When he knocks on the door, the old man asks who is there. "It's me, Death," the white man answers.

"Who you come for?" the old man asks hopefully. "Is it the Mistress?"

"No," says the apparition.

"Is it the Master?"

"No, it's not the master."

"Is it the overseer?"

"No," says the ghost. "I have come for you!"

The terrified old man runs for the woods, and no one ever hears him pray for Death again.

If we think of a white man telling this story, it appears to make fun of the gullible discontented black man. If we think of it as a black man's story, then the story shows that whites will blithely lie and cheat to keep blacks under their yoke. And if we consider the tale as a black man's story retold by a white man, all meanings are possible. What is a poor scholar to do? The answer, I think, is to acknowledge up front that these texts are not one thing or another—they are gumbo, multicultural stew.

Mark Twain, a great fan of Joel Chandler Harris, compared the Brer Rabbit stories to avocados, which he called alligator pears. "One merely eats them for the sake of the salad-dressing," he admiringly remarked.[8] Twain meant that what he liked was not the folktales themselves but the seemingly artless manner in which they were presented. He especially liked the frame story, the portrait of a benign Uncle Remus entertaining an enraptured white child. But the "dressing" Twain and his contemporaries relished has now turned into poison, making most of *Uncle Remus* unpalatable to modern tastes.

To his credit, Jones, unlike Harris, does not bother with salad dressing—until the very end of the book, he simply slices the avocado and hands it over, pit and all. Nor does he pontificate about the origin of the tales or what they may mean. Ever since the first appearance of *Uncle Remus*, scholars have argued over the origins and significance of African American folktales.

In the beginning, one side argued that the tales simply came from Africa while the other insisted that they were borrowed from European sources. And purists persisted in such thinking well into this century. Richard L. Dorson, who collected African American folktales in the 1950s, recalled playing recordings of an informant telling stories first for Melville Herskovits, who exclaimed, "Those are some remarkable African tales!" and then to Stith Thompson, who exclaimed, "Those are some remarkable European tales!"[9] Folklorists now pretty much agree that African American folktales have elements from many different sources, though since the publication of Herskovits's *The Myth of the Negro Past* in 1935 both white and black scholars have stressed the African origins and continuing African elements in black folklore.

The debate has always had political overtones, and it is fascinating to see how the same evidence has been used over the years to support opposing arguments. Nineteenth-century scholars who held that the stories were African regarded them therefore as un-American. If the stories came from somewhere else, of course, then they could not be used as evidence that African Americans resented their oppression. But if the stories originated in Europe, that must mean that blacks had no traditions of their own and simply imitated and childishly distorted the storytelling traditions of their betters. A few early reviews of *Uncle Remus* suggested that African American folktales were critiques of slavery and the plantation system. By the 1960s and '70s some African American scholars insisted that the stories were purely African in origin and could therefore be used as evidence of black cultural independence.[10]

If ever a text could be said to refute all of these arguments, it is Jones's *Gullah Folktales*, a sampler of trickster tales, stories with morals (some, like "De Cat, De Rat, an De Cheese," clearly indebted to Aesop), Gullah versions of European fairy tales ("Stone Soup"), and even a retelling of Chaucer's "Nun's Priest's Tale," the story of a rooster tricked by a fox that was already public property when Chaucer used it in the *Canterbury Tales* in the late 1300s. One could hardly wish for stronger evidence that African American folktales draw motifs from many different cultures.

Unless, of course, Jones's informants were pulling his leg, telling him what they thought he wanted to hear. A few of the tales in *Gullah Folktales* seem specially tailored to appeal to a man like Jones, who was known to come from a family that valued piety above all else. So many of these stories have virtuous messages attached to them that Harold Courlander gives them a separate category in his *Treasury of Afro-American Folklore*—he calls them "moralizing tales." Antebellum Liberty County Georgia was reputed to be so morally upright that, according to one white observer, "not even the Negroes swore."[11] One has to wonder about a statement like that. Had the slaves figured out that the most religious among them were treated better? And, when the younger Jones came back years later and asked them to tell the old stories, did they peg him as a chip off the old block and alter their tales to fit the situation?

If so, they did it with a sense of humor. In "Buh Wolf, Buh Rabbit, an de Butter," the wolf hires the rabbit to hoe his crops, which are in danger of being choked with grass. Rabbit spots a pan of fresh butter at Wolf's house and plots to sneak away and eat it. At this point, the story is similar to the Harris version, and it is easy to see that Wolf represents a wealthy white man and Rabbit a poor black one. In both versions, Rabbit repeatedly leaves his work to nibble at the butter. But in the Jones version Rabbit's excuse seems brilliantly attuned to manipulate a man like Reverend Jones. He tells Wolf that he is a minister and that he needs to leave work in order to baptize a baby. Not only does this excuse work once, it works three times, until Rabbit has managed to consume every ounce of the butter. When Wolf threatens to dock his pay, Rabbit talks so much about the importance of his work as a preacher that Wolf not only pays him full wages but invites him home to supper.

But if Rabbit gets the butter, Wolf gets the last word. Charles Jones could not resist appending four essays in his own pompous, racist voice. After the unmediated pleasures of the rest of the book, these four segments come as something of a shock, and modern readers will undoubtedly wish that Jones had left well enough alone when he finished transcribing the stories. But it was his turn to tell, and the essay was his natural form, just as the story was theirs. These four pieces tell us a good deal about how Jones saw himself, as a superior, well-educated, tolerant man uniquely positioned to record something important that would otherwise be lost. This was not an inaccurate perception. It would be several generations before African Americans would take over as recorders of African American folklore. Those writers who followed in Jones's footsteps, at least until the middle 1930s, were also mostly from the white upper classes—Abigail Christensen, Elsie Clews Parsons, E. C. L. Adams, Julia Peterkin, and Ambrose Gonzales, to name just a few. Later, generations of African American scholars would cast a cold analytical eye on the Eurocentric interpretations that had prevailed for so long. But they could not go back in time to do the fieldwork, to interview nineteenth-century storytellers, and they felt robbed. Jones's work provides some of the best texts we have for studying African American oral culture. Without him, these stories would have been lost—*gone*—forever.

NOTES

1. James William Berry, "Growing Up in the Old South: The Childhood of Charles Colcock Jones, Jr." (Ph.D diss., Princeton University, 1981); quotations are from Charles Colcock Jones, *Religious Instruction of the Negroes*, 1842.

2. Robert Manson Myers, ed., *The Children of Pride: A True Story of Georgia and the Civil War* (New Haven: Yale University Press, 1972). The biographical information in this essay is drawn from Berry and from Myers. See also Charles Edgeworth Jones, "Col. Charles C. Jones, Jr., LL.D., Late of Augusta, GA," *Gulf States Historical Magazine* 1, no. 5 (March 1903): 301–10.

3. R. Bruce Bickley Jr., *Joel Chandler Harris* (Boston: Twayne, 1978), 46–48; C. Vann Woodward, *Origins of the New South, 1877–1913* (Baton Rouge: Louisiana State University Press, 1951), 174. For a fuller discussion of Jones's role as a critic of the New South movement, see Paul M. Baston, *The New South Creed: A Study in Southern Mythmaking* (New York: Knopf, 1970), 142, 154–55, 168, 172.

4. Bickley, *Joel Chandler Harris*, 50.

5. Joseph M. Griska Jr., "In Stead of a 'Gift of Gab': Some New Perspectives on Joel Chandler Harris Biography," in *Critical Essays on Joel Chandler Harris*, ed. Bruce R. Bickley Jr. (Boston: G. K. Hall, 1981), 221. The letter from Harris to Jones is in the Joel Chandler Harris collection at Duke University.

6. Harold Courlander, *A Treasury of Afro-American Folklore: The Oral Literature, Traditions, Recollections, Legends, Tales, Songs, Religious Beliefs, Customs, Sayings, and Humor of People of African Descent in the Americas* (New York: Marlow, 1996).

7. John Szwed and Roger D. Abrahams, *Afro-American Folk Culture* (Philadelphia: Institute for the Study of Human Issues, 1978), xii.

8. Bickley, *Joel Chandler Harris*, 113.

9. Richard M. Dorson, *Handbook of American Folklore* (Bloomington: Indiana University Press, 1983), 16; review of the English edition of *Uncle Remus: His Songs and Sayings*, *Spectator* (2 April 1881): 445–46.

10. Kathleen Light, "Uncle Remus and the Folklorists," in *Critical Essays on Joel Chandler Harris*, 146–47; Bernard Wolfe, "Uncle Remus and the Malevolent Rabbit," in *Critical Essays on Joel Chandler Harris*, 70–84. For an overview of this subject, see Adrienne Lanier Seward, "The Legacy of Early Afro-American Scholarship," in *Handbook of American Folklore*, ed. Richard M. Dorson (Bloomington: Indiana University Press, 1983), 48–56. Important primary texts include Adolph Gerber, "Uncle Remus Traced to the Old World," *Journal of American Folklore*, 1893, and C. Ellis, "Some West African Prototypes of the Uncle Remus Stories," *Popular Science Monthly*, 1891.

11. Berry, "Growing Up in the Old South," 116.

GULLAH FOLKTALES
FROM THE GEORGIA COAST

I.

ONE time Buh Rabbit, him meet Buh
Alligatur, an eh ax um: "Budder, you tek
life berry onconsarne. Enty you come pon
trouble some time?" Buh Alligatur, him
mek answer: "No, Budder, nuttne nebber
bodder me. Me dunno wuh you call trouble.
Me hab plenty er bittle fuh eat. Me sleep
an tek me pledjuh. Wuh mek you tink
trouble kin come topper me?" Buh Rabbit,
him berry cunnin. Eh yent say nuttne. Eh
know Buh Alligatur blan come out de ribber
an sun isself in de broom-grass fiel. Buh
Rabbit, eh laugh oneside to isself an mek
plan to pit trouble on Buh Alligatur.

De nex day, wen de sun hot, Buh Alligatur come out de ribber. Eh so full er fish
an crab eh casely kin crawl. Eh drag isself
trugh de mash, an eh gone in de broom-grass
fiel, and tretch isself in de grass, an fall fas
tersleep. Buh Rabbit bin der watch um all
de time. Buh Rabbit too scheemy. Now
eh pick eh chance. Wen eh tink Buh Alligatur done gone tersleep, eh tiptoe ebber so

1

sofe tell eh come right pon top er Buh Alligatur. Eh notice um close. Eh yeye shet. Eh duh sleep fuh true. Den Buh Rabbit slip back. Eh say to isself: "I guine mek Buh Alligatur know wuh call trouble dis day." Eh trike fire. Eh light one fat pine tick, an eh set fire to de broom-grass all roun an roun de fiel. Buh Alligatur, eh day in de middle fas tersleep. Eh dunno wuh Buh Rabbit up teh. Bimeby de fire, eh biggin fuh roll. Buh Alligatur wake up. Eh see de smoke. Eh yeddy de fire duh commin. Eh dunno wuh fur do. De fire biggin fur bun um. Eh run dis way, de fire meet um. Eh lick back an try tarruh side. De fire meet um day too.

Buh Rabbit, him duh tan off duh watch an duh half kill isself wid laugh. Buh Alligatur holler. Eh holler. Eh holler. Nobody yeddy. Nobody come. Fire ebry side. No way fur um fur go. Eh cant git out. Man! sir! eh mek up eh mine to bus trugh some how. Eh shet eh yeye. Eh cock up eh tail, an yuh eh come straight fur de ribber.

Buh Rabbit, eh fall fur laugh. Eh hoop arter Buh Alligatur, an eh say: "Hey, Budder! wats de time er day? Enty you bin

2

tell me you nebber meet up wid trouble?
You run topper um to-day anyhow."

Buh Alligatur yent hab time fuh mek
answer. Eh yent crack eh teet to Buh Rabbit. Eh jis is bex wid um is eh kin be. Eh
yeye red. Eh tail swinge. Eh gone fuh de
ribber, an eh fall in head ober heel. De
water cool um. Eh ketch eh bref. Den eh
raise isself on de top er de water an eh holler back to Buh Rabbit: "Nummine, Boy,
golong dis time. Me know who mek all dis
trouble fur me. Ef me ebber ketch you
close dis ribber, me guine larne you how ter
come fool long me."

Buh Rabbit faid Alligatur an ribber tell
dis day. From dat day to dis you kin nebber ketch Buh Alligatur sleep fur from de
bank; an de fus time eh yeddy bush crack,
er anyting mek rackit, eh leggo eberyting
an fall right in de water.

II.

Buh Tukrey Buzzud, him yent hab no sense no how. You watch um.

Wen de rain duh po down, eh set on de fench an eh squinch up isself. Eh draw in eh neck, an eh try fur hide eh head, an eh look dat pittyful you rale sorry for um. Eh duh half cry, an eh say to isself: "Num-mine, wen dis rain ober me guine buil house right off. Me yent guine leh dis rain lick me dis way no mo."

Wen de rain done gone, an de win blow, an de sun shine, wuh Buh Tukrey Buzzud do? Eh set on de top er de dead pine tree way de sun kin wam um, an eh tretch out eh wing, an eh tun roun an roun so de win kin dry eh fedder, an eh laugh to isself, an eh say: "Dis rain done ober. Eh yent guine rain no mo. No use fur me fuh buil house now." Caless man dis like Buh Tukrey Buzzud.

HOW BUH COOTER[1] FOOL BUH DEER.*

Buh Deer, him kin outrun all de tarruh creetur. Buh Cooter, him cant go fast no time. Him kin jis creep, an dat all; but him hab plenty er sense.

One day Buh Deer bin a laugh at Buh Cooter becase eh walk so slow. Den Buh Cooter, him git mad, an eh tell Buh Deer dat ef eh does slow eh hab de bes win, an eh bet Buh Deer eh could beat um to de fibe mile pose. Buh Deer, him smile an tuk de bet. Dey gree on nex Monday week fur run de race.

Buh Cooter, him call togedder him fren an tole um bout de bet an wen de race fur run. Eh gaged fibe er um fur help um. Deese yer Cooter am all so much like one anurrer you cant tell one from turrer. So day all come inter cohoot an conclude to fool Buh Deer.

One gone to de fus mile pose on de big road. Anurrer gone to de nex mile pose, an anurrer to de nex: so dat on de day wen

[1]Land Terrapin.
*This and two preceding *Myths* first published in Augusta, Ga., *Chronicle and Constitutionalist* of March 11, 1883.

5

de race fur run, Buh Cooter hab a fren at ebery mile pose. Buh Deer nebber bin know nuttne bout dis plan.

Wen de time come fur run de race, Buh Deer an Buh Cooter bofe stat off togedder. Befo you kin tun roun Buh Deer done gone out uh sight, an lef Buh Cooter in de middle er de road duh laugh to isself. Wen Buh Deer git to de fus mile pose, day was Buh Cooter day head er um. Buh Deer couldnt tell how dat happn. Eh men eh pace. At de nex mile pose day was Buh Cooter a crawlin along. Buh Deer git mad. Eh lay isself out ter eh berry lenk, but befo eh ketch de nex mile pose eh meet Buh Cooter in de road dis a passin er dat pose. Buh Deer jump clean ober um an mek fur de nex mile pose. Eh yent bin want fur bleeve eh own yeye wen eh see Buh Cooter dere done git head er um agin. Eh so mad eh try fuh kick Buh Cooter outer de road, an eh straighten fur de las mile pose. Wen eh git day, eh meet Buh Cooter puffin an er blowin an a leanin up gin de pose duh laugh at um.

An dat de way Buh Cooter fool Buh Deer an win de bet.

IV.

BUH WOLF, BUH RABBIT, AN DE TAR BABY.

Buh Wolf and Buh Rabbit, dem bin lib nabur. De dry drout come. Ebry ting stew up. Water scace. Buh Wolf dig one spring fuh him fuh git water. Buh Rabbit, him too lazy an too scheemy fuh wuk fuh isself. Eh pen pon lib off tarruh people. Ebry day, wen Buh Wolf yent duh watch um, eh slip to Buh Wolf spring, an eh full him calabash long water an cah um to eh house fuh cook long and fuh drink. Buh Wolf see Buh Rabbit track, but eh couldnt ketch um duh tief de water.

One day eh meet Buh Rabbit in de big road, an eh ax um how eh mek out fur water. Buh Rabbit say him no casion fuh hunt water: him lib off de jew on de grass. Buh Wolf quire: "Enty you blan tek water outer me spring?" Buh Rabbit say: "Me yent." Buh Wolf say: "You yis, enty me see you track?" Buh Rabbit mek answer: "Yent me gone to you spring. Must be some edder rabbit. Me nebber bin nigh you spring. Me dunno way you spring day." Buh Wolf no question um no mo; but eh know say eh bin Buh Rabbit fuh true, an eh fix plan fuh ketch um.

7

De same ebenin eh mek Tar Baby, an eh gone an set um right in de middle er de trail wuh lead to de spring, an dist in front er de spring.

Soon a mornin Buh Rabbit rise an tun in fuh cook eh bittle. Eh pot biggin fuh bun. Buh Rabbit say: "Hey! me pot duh bun. Lemme slip to Buh Wolf spring an git some water fuh cool um." So eh tek eh calabash an hop off fuh de spring. Wen eh ketch de spring, eh see de Tar Baby duh tan dist een front er de spring. Eh stonish. Eh stop. Eh come close. Eh look at um. Eh wait fur um fuh mobe. De Tar Baby yent notice um. Eh yent wink eh yeye. Eh yent say nuttne. Eh yent mobe. Buh Rabbit, him say: "Hey titter, enty you guine tan one side an lemme git some water?" De Tar Baby no answer. Den Buh Rabbit say: "Leely Gal, mobe, me tell you, so me kin dip some water outer de spring long me calabash." De Tar Baby wunt mobe. Buh Rabbit say: "Enty you know me pot duh bun? Enty you know me hurry? Enty you yeddy me tell you fuh mobe? You see dis han? Ef you dont go long and lemme git some water, me guine slap you ober." De Tar Baby stan day.

Buh Rabbit haul off an slap um side de head. Eh han fastne. Buh Rabbit try fuh pull eh hand back, an eh say: "Wuh you hole me han fuh? Lemme go. Ef you dont loose me, me guine box de life outer you wid dis tarruh han." De Tar Baby yent crack eh teet. Buh Rabbit hit um, bim, wid eh tarruh han. Dat han fastne too same luk tudder. Buh Rabbit say: "Wuh you up teh? Tun me loose. Ef you dont leggo me right off, me guine knee you." De Tar Baby hole um fas. Buh Rabbit skade an bex too. Eh faid Buh Wolf come ketch um. Wen eh fine eh cant loosne eh han, eh kick de Tar Baby wid eh knee. Eh knee fastne. Yuh de big trouble now. Buh Rabbit skade den wus den nebber. Eh try fuh skade de Tar Baby. Eh say: "Leely Gal, you better mine who you duh fool long. Me tell you, fuh de las time, tun me loose. Ef you dont loosne me han an me knee right off, me guine bus you wide open wid dis head." De Tar Baby hole um fas. Eh yent say one wud. Den Buh Rabbit butt de Tar Baby een eh face. Eh head fastne same fashion luk eh han an eh knee. Yuh de ting now. Po Buh Rabbit done fuh. Eh fastne all side. Eh cant pull loose. Eh

gib up. Eh bague. Eh cry. Eh holler.
Buh Wolf yeddy um. Eh run day. Eh
hail Buh Rabbit: "Hey, Budder! wuh de
trouble? Enty you tell me you no blan
wisit me spring fuh git water? Who calabash dis? Wuh you duh do yuh anyhow?"
Buh Rabbit so condemn eh yent hab one
wud fuh talk. Buh Wolf, him say: "Nummine, I done ketch you dis day. I guine
lick you now." Buh Rabbit bague. Eh
bague. Eh prommus nebber fuh trouble
Buh Wolf spring no mo. Buh Wolf laugh
at um. Den eh tek an loose Buh Rabbit
from de Tar Baby, an eh tie um teh one
spakleberry bush, an eh git switch an eh
lick um tel eh tired. All de time Buh Rabbit bin a bague an a holler. Buh Wolf yent
duh listne ter um, but eh keep on duh pit de
lick ter um. At las Buh Rabbit tell Buh
Wolf: "Dont lick me no mo. Kill me one
time. Mek fire an bun me up. Knock me
brains out gin de tree." Buh Wolf mek
answer: "Ef I bun you up, ef I knock you
brains out, you guine dead too quick. Me
guine trow you in de brier patch, so de brier
kin cratch you life out." Buh Rabbit say:
"Do Buh Wolf, bun me: broke me neck,
but dont trow me in de brier patch. Lemme

10

dead one time. Dont tarrify me no mo."
Buh Wolf yent bin know wuh Buh Rabbit
up teh. Eh tink eh bin guine tare Buh
Rabbit hide off. So, wuh eh do? Eh loose
Buh Rabbit from de spakleberry bush, an
eh tek um by de hine leg, and eh swing um
roun, an eh trow um way in de tick brier
patch fuh tare eh hide an cratch eh yeye
out. De minnit Buh Rabbit drap in de
brier patch, eh cock up eh tail, eh jump, an
eh holler back to Buh Wolf: "Good bye,
Budder! Dis de place me mammy fotch me
up,—dis de place me mammy fotch me
up:" an eh gone befo Buh Wolf kin ketch
um. Buh Rabbit too scheemy.

V.

BUH FOWL-HAWK AN BUH ROOSTER.

Buh Fowl-Hawk, him fly ebry day dis way and dat way ober de lan, an eh cant fine nuttne fuh eat. Eh hail de Sun one time, an eh tell um eh so hongry eh ready fuh drap; dat eh cant git bittle fuh eat; an he dunno wuh fuh do. De Sun, eh say: "Budder, ef you kin ketch me in me bed, me gree fuh fine you in bittle." Buh Hawk tek de greement, an eh try berry hade fuh come pon topper de Sun in eh bed. But ebry time de Sun done git up befo Buh Hawk ketch de place way de Sun sleep. Buh Hawk gib up. Eh dead tired. Den eh tun in an consult Buh Rooster. Buh Rooster yeddy him tale, and den eh say: "Me tell you, Buh Hawk, wuh you better do. You come sleep right ober me back; an wen, soon a mornin, you yeddy me knock me wing togedder and crow, you sail right off fuh de Sun house, an you kin ketch um befo eh git up from eh bed." Buh Hawk do dis es Buh Rooster tell um. Eh come dat ebenin, an eh set on de tree-limb right ober way Buh Rooster duh sleep.

Long befo day duh broke Buh Rooster knock eh wing togarruh an crow. Bless yo

soul! Buh Fowl-Hawk wake up, eh switch
eh tail, eh pitch off de tree, an eh mek fur
de spot way de Sun blan sleep. Eh ketch
um een eh big house. Eh day in eh bed.
Buh Hawk, eh knock to de do. De Sun
say: "Who dat?" Buh Hawk mek answer:
"Duh me." De Sun say: "Who you?"
Buh Hawk say; "Duh me, Budder Hawk."
De Sun quire: "Wuh you want long me?"
Buh Hawk mek answer: "Enty you bin
tell me one day dat ef me kin ketch you in
you bed you guine fine me? Now me done
ketch you in de bed. Gimme de bittle you
prommus me. Me berry hongry." De Sun
bex. Eh wunt come to de do, but eh holler
back to Buh Hawk, an eh say: "You tun
right roun, an you go to de man wuh pint
you to ketch me in me bed, an you tell um
fuh fine you." Buh Hawk rale disappint.
Eh try fuh swade de Sun, but de Sun wunt
listne ter um; and de Sun dribe um way
from him house. Buh Hawk mad, an wen
eh see eh cant git no bittle from de Sun, eh
fly back to Buh Rooster. Buh Rooster, him
ax um: "Me Budder, how you mek out?"
Buh Hawk tell um eh yent mek out wut.
Den eh up an quaint Buh Rooster how de
Sun wouldnt gie um no bittle fuh eat; how

eh dribe um way; an how eh tell um fuh go
back to de man wuh pit um on de trail fuh
ketch um in eh bed, an mek um fine um.
Buh Rooster mek answer: "Budder, me
yent hab no bittle fuh gie you. Me no kin
fine you." Buh Hawk say: "Me dead
tired. Me berry hongry. Me mus hab me
payment." Buh Rooster say: "You cant
git no payment outer me. All me got duh
me wife an me chillun, an me know me yent
guine gie you none er dem." Wen Buh
Hawk see eh cant swade Buh Rooster fuh
fine um, eh try narruh plan. Eh leff Buh
Rooster, an eh sail way up in de element tell
eh done gone in de cloud. All de time eh
duh watch Buh Rooster. Wen Buh Rooster
clean forgit Buh Hawk, an leh eh chillun
play bout een de grass, befo eh know, down
drap Buh Fowl-Hawk, an eh ketch up one
er dem same Buh Rooster chillun. Eh fly
off wid um to one big oak tree, an eh pick
eh bone clean. Buh Rooster holler, but eh
cant tetch Buh Hawk. De chicken sweet.
Buh Hawk feel good. From dat day tell
now, Buh Fowl-Hawk blan pick eh chance
an lib off Buh Rooster chillun.

VI.

BUH TUKREY BUZZUD AN DE KING CRAB.

You notus Buh Tukrey Buzzud. Him lub lamb, an dead cow, an dead horse, an snake, an alligatur, an all kinder varmint. Eh berry lub dead fish too, but eh nebber bodder wid crab. You sabe huccom so? Lemme tell you.

One time one fisher-man bin come from fishin. Eh tek out de good fish, eh tring um on a mash grass, an eh lef in de boat some leely gannet-mullet an catfish wuh eh no want, an one big King Crab wuh eh bin ketch duh ribber. De sun hot. De fish done dead. Bimeby eh smell bad in de boat. Buh Tukrey Buzzud, wuh bin a grine salt way up in de element, scent um, an down eh come. Eh gone in de boat an eh eat up de fish wuh day day. Eh dat greedy eh duh hunt fuh mo. Eh see de King Crab duh squat een de water duh bottom er de boat. Eh tretch open eh wing fuh skade de Crab an mek um come outer de water. Buh Tukrey Buzzud faid water. Eh nebber will wet him foot ef eh kin help. De King Crab see de Buzzud, an eh crawl up long side de boat. Buh Tukrey Buzzud ben ober fuh pick um.

15

De Crab graff Buh Tukrey Buzzud leg wid eh claw. Buh Tukrey Buzzud hop an kick. Eh couldnt mek de Crab leggo. De ting hot um berry bad. Buh Tukrey Buzzud rise wid de Crab duh heng on ter eh leg. Eh sail up in de element. De Crab stick ter um. Buh Tukrey Buzzud try ebry plan fuh shake um off. De Crab wunt loose eh grip. Buh Tukrey Buzzud tun summerset in de sky. Eh flap eh wing. Eh mek all sorter curous motion. Eh cant shake de Crab loose. Bimeby eh try fuh bite de Crab. All ob a sutten, de Crab tek eh tarruh claw, an eh fastne Buh Tukrey Buzzud roun eh neck. Yuh de big trouble now. One claw hole Buh Tukrey Buzzud foot; tarruh claw clamp Buh Tukrey Buzzud roun eh neck. De Bud duh choke. Eh gib up. Eh cant go no fudder. Eh dis leggo ebryting in de element, an eh fall heel ober head plash in de water. De minnit de King Crab fine isself in de ribber, eh loosne eh hole an eh gone der bottom. Buh Tukrey Buzzud mose drown. Eh fedder wet. Eh splutter, eh wabble, an arter awhile eh manage fuh ketch eh bref, an eh mount eh wing, an eh sail off teh one dead libe-oak tree, wuh grow on de bank, an eh set down day an eh pick

eh fedder, an eh watch de blood duh drap
from eh neck an leg, an eh say to isself:
"Me nebber guine bodder long crab gen
long as me lib." An eh nebber did. You
show King Crab to Buh Tukrey Buzzud, an
eh'll leff um. Eh yent guine nigh um. All
eh fambly faid um.

VII.

DE KING, EH DARTER, BUH WOLF, AN BUH RABBIT.

One time er King hab er pooty Darter. Buh Wolf an Buh Rabbit all two bin a spark at um an a cote um. De sanfly bin berry bad. De King tell Buh Wolf an Buh Rabbit de one wuh kin stan de sanfly de longes bedout bresh um way, shill git de gal.

Buh Wolf yent bin so scheemy as Buh Rabbit. Wen dem all was a settin fuh de match, Buh Rabbit, him say: "Gentlemans, my fader had a black horse. Eh had a white spot yuh, and a red spot day; a white spot yuh, and a red spot day; a white spot yuh, and a red spot day." Ebry time eh pint out de place way de spot bin, eh dribe off de sanfly.

Wile dis duh guine on, de sanfly mose eat up Buh Wolf. Eh bleege fur cratch an slap. So Buh Rabbit gain de day, an de King gie um eh Darter.

Buh Wolf, him berry sad, an eh wunt talk. All de lady bin a set in de piazza long de King an eh Darter. Den Buh Rabbit say: "Come, Buh Wolf, leh we broke

18

up. Ef you lemme ride you ter de big gate me guine tun de King Darter ober ter you." Buh Wolf happy. Eh gree fuh leh Buh Rabbit ride um. Buh Rabbit light on eh back. Eh hab spur on. Buh Wolf dunno nuttne bout dis. Soon es Buh Rabbit git on Buh Wolf back, eh clamp eh leg onder Buh Wolf belly, an eh clap spur ter Buh Wolf. Buh Wolf rare up. Eh jump. Eh kick. Eh leddown. Eh try ebry way fuh trow Buh Rabbit. Buh Rabbit stick ter eh back, an wunt fall off. De mo Buh Wolf rare up an kick an pitch, de wus Buh Rabbit spur um. Wen eh fine eh cant trow Buh Rabbit, eh tek de big road an lean fuh de gate. Buh Rabbit stick de spur in um ebry jump. Buh Wolf run. Eh run. Eh holler. Eh holler. Buh Rabbit duh set on eh back an duh spur um, an duh look dess as happy an content as eh kin be. Wen dey guine tru de big gate, Buh Rabbit light off eh back an jump on top de gate pose. Buh Wolf cant stop run. Eh gone. Buh Rabbit shet de gate, an tun back, an jine de compny, an tek eh bride.

VIII.

BUH PATTRIDGE AN BUH RABBIT.

Buh Pattridge and Buh Rabbit jine compny fuh kill cow. Wen dey done kill um, dey share de meat equel. Buh Pattridge tek one half; Buh Rabbit, him tek tarruh half. Buh Pattridge tote him share home, an cook some, an gen um to him chillun. Buh Rabbit, him tay buhhine an watch him share. Wen Buh Pattridge an him chillun done eat dem belly full, Buh Pattridge gone back to de place way de cow bin kill. Eh meet Buh Rabbit duh siddown day duh wait fuh hire somebody fuh cahr him meat ter him house. Buh Pattridge, him want mo meat. Eh up an tell Buh Rabbit: "Dat cow meat no good. Me cook some an gen to me chillun, an eh kill two er um." Buh Rabbit say: "Eh yent." Buh Pattridge say: "Me tell you eh yiz. Me bin eat some too, an eh mek me feel berry bad. Rattlesnake must a bin trike dat cow an pizen um." Den Buh Pattridge fall on de groun, an flutter, flutter, flutter, dis like eh bin guine fuh dead. Buh Rabbit tink say de pizen meat been a wuk in um, an eh hop off, an eh fetch water, an eh trow um in Buh Pattridge face. Wen Buh Pattridge sorter vive, Buh Rabbit tell um eh no want de meat, dat eh guine leff um. Den Buh Rabbit wish Buh Pattridge de time er day, an gone teh him house. Soon as Buh Rabbit git outer yearin, Buh Pattridge whistle fuh him chillun. De gang all bin in de bush duh watch. Den dey all run up an cahr de meat to dem house, an cook um an eat um.

De meat bin good, an Buh Pattridge only do dat fuh fool Buh Rabbit an git him share too.

IX.

DE OLE MAN AN DE GALLINIPPER.

An ole man bin a hunt roccoon in de wood. Eh hab eh dog fuh tree de coon, an eh hatchich fuh chop down de tree. De dog bark. De ole man gone ter um. Eh look up de tree fuh see de coon. Steader de coon, er big Gallinipper bin a settin in de crotch er de sweet-gum. De tree so big de ole man cant retch round um wid bofe eh arm. De dog bark at de Gallinipper. Eh bark. Eh bark. De Gallinipper git bex. Eh light off de tree fuh bite de dog. De dog holler an run roun de tree. De Gallinipper miss eh lick, an dribe eh bill trugh de tree tell de pint come out on tarruh side. De ole man try fuh chop off de een er de Gallinipper bill. Wen de Gallinipper see wuh de ole man up teh, eh rare back an try fur pull eh bill outer de tree. Eh fastne so tight eh couldnt git um out, but eh strain so hebby eh drag de tree up by de root. De ole man dat scade eh drop eh hatchich, eh leff eh dog der wood, and eh lean fur home.

X.

BUH SPARRUH.

Buh Sparruh, him berry leetle, but him lub fur brag. Eh yent much fur wuk.

One time de Bluefinch, de Trasher, de Red-Bud, de Jay-Bud, de Pattridge, and de Sparruh all come inter cohoot ter plant tetter[1] and see who kin raise de bigges. Wen de tetter done mek an dig, all de bud collec togarruh, an ebry one fotch a tetter ter show wuh kind a crop eh mek. De Crow bin de judge. Eh look ober all de tetter, an wen eh fine Buh Sparruh no bin bring none, eh ax Buh Sparruh: "Way you tetter?" Buh Sparruh biggin fur brag, an eh say: "Me tetter, him heap bigger den any me see. Me farruh befo me blan plant tetter, an him tetter bigger ner de calf er me leg. Me kin beat me farruh raise tetter. Me yent bin bring no tetter wid me case me no want fur mek me fren feel bad." Tarruh bud say: "Nummine, you go fetch you tetter. Leh we see um." Wen Buh Sparruh fine dem all bent pon mek um show eh tetter, eh say: "Well, wait pon top me. Me guine git me tetter." Buh Sparruh gone, an de bud all wait. Dem wait tell dem tired, an Buh

[1]Sweet potatoes.

23

Sparruh no come back. Den Buh Crow, wuh bin de judge, sen Buh Bluefinch fur fine Buh Sparruh, an see wuh eh duh do. Buh Bluefinch meet Buh Sparruh duh pick seed in one ole fiel. Eh hail um: "Hey! Buh Sparruh! wuh mek you no come back? All de tarruh bud duh wait top you fur show you tetter." Buh Sparruh rare isself back, an eh mek answer: "You go tell Buh Crow an de tarruh gentlemans me tetter so big me cant tote um."

Buh Sparruh lie. Eh dis bin a brag. Eh yent nebber bin plant no tetter.

XI.

BUH ALLIGATUR AN BUH MASH-HEN.

Buh Alligatur nebber does trubble Buh Mash-hen an eh chillun. Enty, heap a time, you see Buh Mash-hen duh ketch fiddler on de ribber bank close by way Buh Alligatur duh feed, an Buh Alligatur yent lick at um wid eh tail, ner skade um? You know huccum dis? Ef you dunno, lemme tell you.

One time Buh Alligatur, him been er eat crab. Him bin hab one teet wuh hab hole in um. Dat teet duh hot um berry bad. Buh Alligatur blan chaw up crab, shell an all. Wen eh der eat dem crab, one er de claw fastne in him rotten teet, and hot um so bad eh mek um holler. Eh cant do nuttne cept open eh jaw an moan. Eh foot yent long nough fuh pick de claw out.

Wile eh bin a moan an suffer, Buh Mash-hen pass by. Buh Alligatur hail um an tell um wuh happne, and mek um sensible how bad de claw duh hot um, an how eh yent hab de power fuh git um out, an eh bague um fuh pull de ting out wid eh bill. Buh Mash-hen yeddy um, but eh fade fur trus eh head between Buh Alligatur jaw. Eh spicion say Buh Alligatur guine trick um, an kill um, an eat um, an eh tell Buh Alligatur him too scheemy. But Buh Alligatur, him schway to Buh Mash-hen dat eh yent guine trubble um, an dat ef eh would bleege um an pick de ting out, eh would be fren ter um an eh fambly all dem life, an mek all dem tarruh Alligatur fren too.

Wen Buh Mash-hen see Buh Alligatur duh bague so harde, an wen eh fine out eh bin der tell de trute, eh tek pity on um, an eh pit eh head in eh mouf an eh pull out de crab-claw, wuh fastne in eh teet, wid eh bill.

Dat ease Buh Alligatur, an eh tell Buh Mash-hen heap er tenky. An eh mek all eh quaintunce sensible er de big faber wuh Buh Mash-hen bin done ter um.

Buh Alligatur, him keep eh wud. Ebber sence, Buh Mash-hen kin walk bout de mash an de ribber, an buil nes, an ketch fiddler an shrimp all round Buh Alligatur, an eh yent try fuh bodder um.

Dat de way Buh Alligatur an Buh Mash-hen come fur lib togerruh luk same fambly.

XII.

BUH FOWL-HAWK AN BUH TUKREY BUZZUD.

Time bin berry harde. Bittle oncommon scace. Buh Fowl-hawk an Buh Tukrey Buzzud, dem bin a sail backwud and forrud in de element, duh look fuh see wuh dem kin pick up fur eat. Es dem pass one a nurruh, Buh Fowl-hawk, him ax Buh Tukrey Buzzud how him mek out. Buh Tukrey Buzzud mek answer dat eh yent mek out wut; dat half de time eh cant fine nuttne fuh eat; dat eh so hongry eh mos ready fuh perish; but dat eh mek up eh mine ter keep on guine, an ter wait on de Lord. Den eh quire ob Buh Fowl-hawk how him duh git long dis yer tight time. Buh Fowl-hawk, him switch eh tail, an eh say him smarte nough fuh git him libbin; dat him dont lack fuh bittle; dat Lord er no Lord, him manage fuh fine all him want fuh eat.

Wid dat dem part compny, an gone dem own couse.

Bimeby dem sail pass one anurrer gen, an Buh Fowl-hawk, him call to Buh Tukrey Buzzud, an him say: "Enty me bin tell you me hab no trouble fuh fine bittle wenebber

me want um? You see dat black chicken
down yander? Me guine ketch um now fuh
me dinner."

Wid dat, eh leff Buh Tukrey Buzzud, an
eh mek eh lunge fuh kibber de chicken.
Stidder eh bin one chicken, eh tun out fuh
bin er sharp-pinted stump; an befo Buh
Fowl-hawk fine out de diffunce, an kin check
eh speed, eh hit eh bres gin de stump an kill
ehself.

Two, tree day arter dat, Buh Tukrey Buzzud bin a sail ober de same groun, an eh
cotch de scent er someting dead. Eh fole
eh wing an eh come down. Wen eh come
fuh fine out, eh see Buh Fowl-hawk duh led
down dead. Den eh say: "Enty me bin
tell you eh heap better ter wait on de Lord
stidder trus ter you own luck? You wouldnt
yeddy me, an you see wuh happne. Now
me tun come, an you flesh guine ile me
bade." Wid dat, eh eat up Buh Fowl-hawk.

"De man wuh trus in ehself," moralized
Daddy Sandy, "guine fail; wile dem dat
wait topper de Lord will hab perwision mek
fur um."

XIII.

BUH WOLF AN BUH RABBIT.

Buh Wolf and Buh Rabbit bin a cote de same Gal. De Gal bin rich an berry pooty. Dem tuk tun fuh wisit um. Buh Rabbit, him gone der mornin, and Buh Wolf, him gone der ebenin. De Gal harde fuh mek up eh mine. Eh sorter courage bofe er um. One mornin Buh Rabbit bin a mek fun er Buh Wolf ter de Gal, an eh tell um say Buh Wolf yent duh nuttne mo den eh far-ruh ridin horse.

Wen Buh Wolf pay him wisit de same ebenin, de Gal tell um wuh Buh Rabbit bin say bout um. De ting mek Buh Wolf bex, an eh say Buh Rabbit lie, an eh guine fetch Buh Rabbit ter de Gal an mek um tek back dat big wud befo eh face.

Buh Wolf leff de Gal an gone straight ter Buh Rabbit house. Buh Rabbit bin spicion say de Gal guine tell Buh Wolf wuh him bin say bout um; an eh know, wen Buh Wolf yeddy, dat eh boun fur tackle um bout um. So Buh Rabbit, him fix eh plan.

Wen Buh Wolf git ter Buh Rabbit house, eh fine um all shet up. Eh look same luk nobody bin day. Eh knock ter de do. Eh

knock. Eh knock. No ansur. Eh gone
ter de winder. Eh shake um. Nobody mek
ansur. Den eh holler: "Buh Rabbit, Buh
Rabbit!" Arter a while eh yeddy er leely
woice eenside say: "Who dat?" Buh Wolf
ansur: "Duh me, Buh Wolf." Buh Rabbit
say: "Wuh you want, Buh Wolf?" Buh
Wolf, him say: "Lemme come in, Buh Rabbit; me bleege fuh see you on tickler bidness." Buh Rabbit, him mek ansur: "Buh
Wolf, me cant see you now; me berry sick;
me day in me bed; me too weak fuh open
de do." Buh Wolf say: "Buh Rabbit, you
mus lemme in: you de only man wuh kin
ten ter de bidness wuh bring me yuh." Buh
Rabbit try fuh pit um off. Eh tell um eh
hab high feber, an eh cant rise; dat eh
back bin er hot um so bad eh cant tun in eh
bed. But Buh Wolf cist so strong, Buh
Rabbit slip to de do, an eh draw de bolt, an
eh tiptoe back ter eh bed, an den eh say:
"Well Budder, ef you mus see me, bad off
es me yiz, come in." Wen Buh Wolf come
in, eh fine Buh Rabbit kibber up in eh bed,
duh pant an duh moan berry pittiful. Buh
Wolf tan by de bed, an eh ax Buh Rabbit:
"Enty you tell de Gal, wuh we bin a cote,
say me bin nuttne but you farruh ridin

horse?" Buh Rabbit say: "Me nebber did." Buh Wolf say: "You yiz bin tell um so." Buh Rabbit say: "Me yent." Den Buh Wolf schway: "De Gal done tell um say Buh Rabbit sisso, an eh bleebe de Gal." Buh Rabbit run Buh Wolf down dat eh nebber bin nuse no sich wud. Den Buh Wolf say: "Ef you nebber bin say no sich wud, you mus git up an go long me, an knowledge befo de Gal dat you nebber bin sisso." Buh Rabbit hole back. Eh say eh too weak fuh git outer de bed, and dat ef eh did get up eh too weak fuh walk ter de Gal house. But Buh Wolf foce um. Eh say: "You got ter go. Me guine help you outer de bed, an ef you cant tek you foot, me guine tote you." Wen Buh Rabbit fine no chance fur um fuh dodge no mo, an dat Buh Wolf boun fuh mek um go, eh git Buh Wolf fuh help um outer de bed. Arter eh git on de flo, Buh Rabbit sorter faint way. Buh Wolf tek um up an cahr um ter de do, an fan um. Buh Rabbit bin a play possum all de time. Wen eh come too, Buh Wolf liff um up an pit um on eh back. Buh Rabbit say: "Hole on, Buh Wolf, me cant set on you back dout fall off: me mus hab someting fuh steady me; you mus gimme someting fuh

31

me fuh hole on ter. Yuh me farruh ole saddle an bridle. Lemme pit dem on you, an
den me tink me kin manage fuh go long wid
you." Buh Wolf, him yent spicion nuttne,
an eh tan still an leh Buh Rabbit pit de
saddle an bridle on um. Onbeknowinst ter
Buh Wolf, Buh Rabbit slip behind de do an
pit on er pair er keen spur. Den Buh Wolf
help um on eh back, an state fuh trot fuh de
Gal house. Buh Rabbit say: "Buh Wolf,
dont go so fas: me so weak me cant hole on;
you mus walk." Buh Wolf, him haky ter
um, an eh come down ter a walk. Wen
dem retch de abnue wuh lead from de big
road ter de house way de Gal lib, dem shum
all dress een white duh settin in de piazza.
Soon es dem pass tru de big gate, Buh Rabbit, him gedder de range in eh han, an eh
slap spur to Buh Wolf. Buh Wolf say:
"You fool, wuh you duh do?" an eh rare an
pitch an try fuh trow Buh Rabbit off. Buh
Rabbit stick on, an eh clap de spur wus an
wus ter Buh Wolf. Wen Buh Wolf fine
out eh cant do nuttne, eh keep de abnue
straight fur de house. Wen dem duh nigh
de house Buh Rabbit holler ter de Gal:
"Wuh me bin tell you? Yuh me come pon
me farruh ridin horse," an eh rip spur een

Buh Wolf an eh hole um tight. De spur hot Buh Wolf so bad eh couldnt do nuttne but run. Buh Rabbit tun um dest by de piazza, an eh light off eh back, an eh run up ter de Gal, an eh say: "Wuh you tink er me farruh ridin horse?" Buh Wolf so painful, so bex, an so shame, eh keep on run, an eh nebber come back fur see de Gal no mo.

Buh Rabbit, him too scheemy fuh Buh Wolf. Wen de Gal notus how smate Buh Rabbit bin, an how eh mek good eh big wud, eh gen um eh han, an, leetle while arter, dem bin git marry.

XIV.

BUH WOLF AN DE TWO DINNER.

Buh Wolf, him binner inwite ter two dinner de same day an de same time: one gen
by Cooter Bay, an de tarruh by John Bay.
Dem bin bredder, an dem lib on two seprite
road wuh jine at de fork. Buh Wolf, him
so greedy him cept bofe inbitation. Wen
de time come fuh go, eh dress ehself up an
eh light out. Wen eh git ter de place way
de road fork, eh stop an eh consider. Eh
want fuh tek bofe road an go ter de two dinner. Eh cant tek one an leff tarruh. Eh
gone down one road; eh tun back; eh tan
ter de fork. Eh tek tarruh road; eh come
back ter de fork; eh tan day gen. Eh state
off; eh tun back. Eh state off gen; eh tun
back gen. Eh cant mek up eh mine which
dinner fuh tek an which dinner fuh leff. Eh
hanker arter bofe. Eh wase eh time. Wile
dis bin a guine on, de people bin a eat at
bofe de dinner.

Bimeby yuh come some er dem, wuh bin
eat dinner wid Cooter Bay, duh mek dem
way home. Dem see Buh Wolf duh tan in
de fork er de road, an dem hail um, an dem
say: "Hi! Buh Wolf, wuh you duh do

34

yuh?" Buh Wolf, him mek answer: "Me guine ter Cooter Bay fuh dine long um." Den dem tell um say de dinner done ober; dat dem jist come from day, an dat dem bin hab plenty er good bittle fuh eat. Buh Wolf rale cut down case eh loss one dinner.

Eh hop off an mek fuh John Bay house fuh git de tarruh dinner. Eh yent bin gone no destant befo eh meet dem people duh comin back wuh bin gone fuh eat dinner long John Bay. Dem tell um de dinner done ober, an eh mights well tun back. Buh Wolf outdone. Eh so greedy eh couldnt mek up eh mine which dinner fuh tek. Eh tink eh guine git all two, an eh yent git none. Eh gone home dat bex an hongry eh ready fuh kill ehself.

People wuh wunt mek up dem mine in time wuh dem mean fuh do guine git leff.

XV.

Buh Owl, him bin a great music-meker. Him an Buh Rooster bin good fren. Heap er bud blan wisit Buh Rooster house fuh yeddy music an fuh dance. Buh Owl, him sing so well an eh pick de banjo so clear, nobody kin listen ter um an keep eh foot still; but eh no wan leh nobody shum wen eh duh sing an play. Buh Rooster, him always blan hab a dark room fuh Buh Owl fuh set in wen eh duh play fuh de bud. Lamp day in day, but eh hab shade on um. Buh Owl kin see de bud wuh duh dance, but de bud, dem cant see Buh Owl. Buh Owl, him faid light, an eh yent der bole bud no how.

One ebenin Buh Owl bin a sing an play oncommon well fuh de bud at Buh Rooster house fuh dance. De pahler bin full, but dem yent bin know who dat bin a mek de music. Buh Rooster, him bin prommus Buh Owl dat eh yent guine tell who duh sing an play. Wen dem all bin dance tel dem tired, dem all bague Buh Rooster fuh show dem de man wuh bin mek sich pooty music fuh dem fuh dance long. Buh Rooster say him cant. Dem keep on bague, tel, at lenk, Buh Roos-

36

ter gone in tarruh room, an eh tek de shade
offer de lamp. Wen dem look pon topper
Buh Owl, eh yeye so big, an eh yez cock up
so high, eh skade de people, an dem all holler
an run.

Buh Owl, him berry bex case Buh Rooster
broke eh wud, an he fall out wid Buh Rooster. From dat day Buh Owl hate Buh
Rooster, eh wife, an eh chillun. Wenebber,
duh night, eh yeddy any er um duh crow er
der fix ehself topper eh roose, eh mek fuh
de place an eat um up. Eh yent do, in dis
wul, fuh man fuh ceive eh fren.

XVI.

BUH LION AN BUH GOAT.

Buh Lion bin a hunt, an eh spy Buh Goat duh leddown topper er big rock duh wuk eh mout an der chaw. Eh creep up fuh ketch um. Wen eh git close ter um eh notus um good. Buh Goat keep on chaw. Buh Lion try fuh fine out wuh Buh Goat duh eat. Eh yent see nuttne nigh um ceptin de nekked rock wuh eh duh leddown on. Buh Lion stonish. Eh wait topper Buh Goat. Buh Goat keep on chaw, an chaw, an chaw. Buh Lion cant mek de ting out, an eh come close, an eh say: "Hay! Buh Goat, wuh you duh eat?" Buh Goat skade wen Buh Lion rise up befo um, but eh keep er bole harte, an eh mek ansur: "Me duh chaw dis rock, an ef you dont leff, wen me done long um me guine eat you." Dis big wud sabe Buh Goat. Bole man git outer diffikelty way coward man lose eh life.

XVII.

Buh Bear, him tired lib wid eh farruh an
eh fambly, an eh tell eh farruh eh guine way
fuh mek eh own libbin, an eh want um fuh
gem wuhebber eh hab wuh cummin ter um
from de fambly property. Eh farruh an eh
murrer try fuh swade um fuh stay long dem,
but eh say eh mek up eh mine fuh go. Den
eh farruh tell um eh yent hab nuttne fuh
gem cept sebbn loaf er bread. Buh Bear,
him berry disappint; but wen eh see eh
yent guine git nuttne mo, eh gree fuh tek
um. Eh farruh tell um: "De man wuh eat
any er dat bread long you will hab fuh
rastle long you fuh sebbn year." Buh Bear
cahr eh bread, an gone der wood, an mek
camp fuh ehself. Wen eh bin er eat de
bread, Buh Tiger come long an bague um fuh
some. Buh Bear say: "Buh Tiger, ef you eat
any er dis yer bread, you haffer rastle long
me fuh sebbn year." Buh Tiger, him answer:
"Me willin: me hongry; gimme de bread."
Den Buh Bear gen um some, an eh eat um.
Befo dem part Buh Tiger tell Buh Bear way
him house yiz, and gree fuh rastle long um
de nex mornin. Buh Bear say: "Berry well:

39

me guine come ter you house by de time de sun git up, an you will haffer rastle long me."

Soon a mornin Buh Bear gone ter Buh Tiger house an knock ter de do. Buh Tiger come out in er hurry, an dey graff hold er one anurrer. Buh Bear fling Buh Tiger; an befo eh leh um git up, eh box um side er de head.

Nex day Buh Bear come gen same time, and Buh Tiger meet um, an dem rastle, an Buh Bear fling um an hit um side er de head, same place way eh bin knock um de day befo. Nex day same ting. Nex day same ting. Nex day same ting. De six mornin, wen Buh Bear knock ter Buh Tiger do, Buh Tiger yent come out. Eh sen eh wife fuh say eh bin berry sick. Buh Bear say eh mus come out. Eh wife tell um; an arter Buh Tiger fine out Buh Bear yent guine leff, eh come out. Eh head swell way Buh Bear bin a box um. Buh Tiger look bad. Buh Bear hole um gen an eh trow um berry easy, an den eh box um gen in de same ole place sider eh head, way eh bin a knock um befo, an wuh swell. Eh hot Buh Tiger so bad eh holler. De nex mornin, wen Buh Bear come, Buh Tiger bin in eh bed. Eh head tie up, an eh wife bin a nuss um. Eh couldnt rastle long Buh Bear no mo. Buh Bear, him shame um, an mek um leff eh house. Den Buh Bear mobe in an mek ehself satify.

Buh Bear fine out dat de bread wuh eh farruh bin gen um, an wuh eh hardly bin want fuh tote long um, done um a heap er good, an git um er nice house fuh lib een.

"Wenebber," added old Daddy Smart, "you farruh gie you anyting, tek um, an tenky. You suttenly will fine out dat wuh eh gie you will do you no harm, but eh will fetch good luck ter you."

XVIII.

BUH MONKEY AN DE BULL-DOG.

Ebry body cept Buh Monkey bin full er trouble. On ebry side you yeddy nuttne cept bout trouble. Trouble yuh, trouble day, trouble ebry way. Buh Monkey tell eh wife eh wonder wuh dis ting duh wuh ebry body bin a talk bout, an wuh dem all duh call trouble. Him say him cant tell. Den Buh Monkey mek up eh mine fuh go teh de Debble, an fine out from um. Eh gone. Eh ketch de Debble duh eat eh brukwus; an eh ax um huccum ebry body hab trouble cept him. An eh leh de Debble know say him wan fine out wuh dis ting duh wuh bin a bodder ebry body, an wuh ebry body call trouble. De Debble tell um fuh go een de kitchin an wait topper um, an wen eh done eh brukwus him will come out an mek um sensible bout dis ting wuh call trouble. Buh Monkey gone ter de kitchin, an tek one chair an mek ehself saterfy. Eh jaw duh run water, fuh eh tink ter ehself de Debble guine gem some nice brukwus. Eh wait day sich a lenk er time, an no brukwus come. Den de Debble come outer de big house duh fetch er bag een eh han. De

42

bag done tie up. Eh gen de bag ter Buh
Monkey, an eh tell um: "Trouble day een
dis yer bag. You cahr um tel you git een
de middle er de ole fiel, an den you open um,
an you guine fine out wuh call trouble."
Big fiel bin all roun an roun de house. Not
a tree nur a stump bin in dat fiel. Buh
Monkey tek de bag. Eh hebby. Eh state
fuh home duh tote um. Eh tired befo eh
retch de middle er de fiel. Wen eh ketch
de middle er de fiel, eh top, an eh onloose de
bag. Bless God! out jump one Bull-Dog,
an eh tek right arter Buh Monkey. Eh run.
Eh run. Eh holler. Eh holler. De Dog
day right arter um duh try fuh bite um.
Wen Buh Monkey git ter de wood, eh state
fuh clime de fus tree eh come teh. De Dog
so close behine um eh snap at um an bite off
eh tail. Buh Monkey leff eh tail een de
dog mouf, an gone up de tree. Eh fine one
crotch, an eh seddown duh pant an der cry.
Eh skade so tell eh scacely kin keep eh
seat. Eh tail duh bleed. De Dog sed down
onder de tree, an watch um, an wait fur um
fuh come down. Buh Monkey faid fuh
come down. Ebry time dat Buh Monkey
mek motion fuh come down, de Dog show eh
teet an growl. Night come, and Buh Mon-

key, him day up de tree. Eh fine out fuh true wuh call trouble. Eh dat tired, an sore, an skade, eh dunno wuh fuh do. Bout middle der night de Dog hongry, an gone home fuh eat eh bittle. Buh Monkey slip down de tree an mek track fuh him house. Wen eh meet eh wife an chillun, an show um eh tail wuh bite off, an tell um wuh eh bin tru, dem all mek er great miration, an dem all conclude dem know nuff bout trouble, an yent want see um no mo. Bad plan fuh people fuh hunt trouble wen trouble yent der hunt dem.

XIX.

Buh Elephant, him bin know Buh Rooster berry well. Dem blan roam togerrur, an Buh Rooster blan wake Buh Elephant duh mornin, so eh kin hunt eh bittle befo de jew dry.

Dem bin a talk togerrur one day, an Buh Elephant, him bet Buh Rooster say him kin eat longer ner him. Buh Rooster, him tek de bet, an dem tun in nex mornin, wen de sun jis bin a git up, fuh see who guine win de bet. Buh Elephant, him gedder leaf an grass, an eat an eat tel eh full an cant eat no mo. Buh Rooster, him sarche de grass fuh seed an wurrum, an eh pick an eat. Wen Buh Elephant done full, an der tan onder de tree duh flop eh yez, eh see Buh Rooster, dist es spry, duh walk bout an der swaller seed an grasshopper an wurrum same luk eh dis biggin fuh eat. Buh Elephant gib up. Eh fine eh yent de man wid de bigges belly wuh kin eat de longes.

XX.

DE PO MAN AN DE SNAKE.

One po Man bin er mek eh libbin long
split shingle an cut timber in de swamp.
Him hab wife, but no chillun. Ebry day,
from sunrise tel sundown, eh day in de
swamp der cut. Try eh bes, eh scacely kin
mek bread fuh eat.

One berry big Snake—de farruh er all
dem tarruh snake wuh lib in de swamp—
notus de po man. Eh see how hard eh wuk
an how little eh mek, and eh tek pity on um.
One ebenin, dis befo de po man knock off
wuk, dis snake crawl up ter de log way de
man bin er chop, an eh say: "Budder, how
you der mek out?" De man mek answer:
"Me yent mek out wut. Me der wuk in
dis swamp from sunrise tel dark, day een an
day out, an try me bes, me scacely kin mek
bittle nough fuh me an me wife fuh eat."
Den de snake, him say: "Me sorry fuh you,
an me willin fuh help you." De man tenk
um, an ax um how eh guine help um. De
snake say: "You got any chillun?" De
man say: "No." De snake quire: "You hab
wife?" De man say: "Yes." De snake
say: "Kin you keep secret from you wife?"

46

De man mek answer say eh kin. Buh Snake tell um eh faid fuh truss um; but wen de man bague de snake berry hard fuh try um, de snake gree fuh do so. Den de snake tell um eh guine gen um some money nex day, but eh mussne tell eh wife way eh git de money. De man mek strong prommus, and so dem part.

De nex day, jis befo de po man done task, de snake crawl up. Eh belly an eh mouf puff out. Eh spit two quart er silber money on de groun dist in front er de po man, an eh say: "You member wuh me bin tell you las ebenin? Well, yuh some money me fotch fuh help you. Tek um, but member ef you tell you wife way you git um, er who gen um ter you, eh yent guine do you no good, an you guine dead a po man." De man so glad fuh git de money eh say: "Tenky, tenky, tenky, me budder; me neber guine tell nobody way me git all dis money. Arter eh leff de swamp fuh gone home, de snake spicion say eh bin guine go back on eh prommus an tell eh wife: so eh mek up eh mine fuh foller um an see wuh happne.

Eh bin dark wen eh retch de man house. Eh crawl up, an eh leddown dist onder de winder, way him kin yeddy all de wud wuh talk in de house. De man wife bin a tun roun an der cook supper. Arter him an eh husbun done eat, eh husbun say: "Me bin hab big luck ter-day: looker dis money." Den eh pull out de silber and spread um on de table. Eh wife stonish. Eh wife glad, an eh say: "Tell me way you bin git all dis money." De man say: "Fren gen um ter me." Eh wife say: "Wuh fren?" De man say him prommus no fuh tell. De wife say but eh mus tell um, an eh bague so hard tel de man done furgit eh prommus, an eh up an mek um sensible how de ting all happne. Den eh wife say: "Dat snake must hab eh belly full er silber money, an me tell you wuh you do ter-morruh. Wen de snake come fuh talk long you, you pick you chance an chop eh head off long you ax, an tek all de money outer um." Eh husbun gree fur do dist is him say.

Buh Snake, him yeddy ebry wud dem talk, an eh gone to him house in de swamp berry bex case de man wuh eh bin befren shouldder gone back on eh prommus and mek bad bargain fuh kill um.

De nex day de man watch fuh de snake. Wen de sun duh lean fuh down, an de man bin a try fuh split one big log, Buh Snake

48

crawl up long sider de log an show ehself ter de man. Dem talk togerrur; an de snake ax de man: "You bin show you wife de money wuh me bin gen you?" De man answer: "Yes, me yiz." An den eh ax um: "You bin tell you wife way you bin git um?" De man say: "No." De snake ax um gen: "You sho you no bin tell um you git um long me?" De man say: "Me tell you one time ready. Wuh mek you ax me dat questun gen? You tink me duh lie?" Wid dat, eh mek eh lick fuh chop de snake head off. De snake bin hab eh yeye on um, an eh draw back gin de log. De ax miss de snake, an glance back off de log an cut de man own leg off. De po man holler fuh somebody fuh come fuh help um. Eh day way in de swamp out er yearin, an noboddy yeddy. Wen eh duh bleed ter det, an dis befo eh dead, Buh Snake, him say ter um: "Enty me bin tell you, wen me gen you dat silber money, ef you tell you wife way you git um you guine dead one po man? You prommus me you guine keep de secret. Steader dat, you gone home ter you wife, an you show um de money, an you tell um way you git um. Mo na dat: you an him fix plan fuh kill me wuh bin you fren, an rob me outer wuh money me hab leff. Now you see de jedgment wuh come topper you. In try fuh chop me head off, you cut you own foot off. You gwine dead in dis yer wood. No man ner ooman gwine fine you. Buzzud gwine eat you."

Eh happne dis is de snake say. De man broke eh wud, an eh dead a po man.

Anybody wuh gwine back on eh prommus, an try fuh harm de pusson wuh done um a faber, sho ter meet up wid big trouble.

XXI.

A leely Gal bin a gwine home. Eh come
ter de ribber bank, an no boat day fuh him
fuh git cross. Eh dunno wuffer do. Eh
seddown. Eh cry. Day binner gwine. Alligatur yeddy um, an eh come day, an eh ax
de leely Gal wuh de matter. De leely Gal
tell um. Den de Alligatur say: "Ef you
prommus no fuh tell who cahr you ober de
ribber, me will pit you cross." De leely Gal
prommus, an de Alligatur tek um on eh
back and ferry um ober all safe.

De nex day de Alligatur duh sun ehself
on de ribber bank, an eh yeddy er woice
say: "Yaller-belly Alligatur ferry me ober.
Yaller-belly Alligatur ferry me ober." Eh
listne. Eh tink say de leely Gal bin a talk,
an dat eh bin broke eh prommus. Eh notus
close, an wen eh yeddy de woice gen eh see
er Blue-Jay bin er talk um een de tree. Dat
same Blue-Jay bin day de ebenin befo, an
bin er see an er yeddy all wuh happne, but de
leely Gal an de Alligatur nebber bin know.

De Jay-Bud keep a holler: "Yaller-belly
Alligatur ferry me ober." De Alligatur call

to de Jay-Bud, an eh quire: "Wudder dat
you say?" An de Jay-Bud keep a sing:
"Yaller-belly Alligatur ferry me ober." Alligatur, him say: "Me hard er yearin. Come
close, so me kin yeddy you song." De Bud
fly down dist by Buh Alligatur, an eh sing
gen: "Yaller-belly Alligatur ferry me ober."
Buh Alligatur yeddy um berry well, but eh
so bex say de Bud done fine out, an der
talk eh secret, dat eh want fuh kill um sho.
So eh say gen: "Me tell you me deef; come
close; set on me nose, so me kin yeddy wuh
you duh sing." De fool Bud come an light
on eh nose, an eh holler gen: "Yaller-belly
Alligatur ferry me ober." De wud yent leff
eh mouf befo Buh Alligatur trow open him
mouf an ketch um, an chaw de life outer um.

Bad plan fur stranger fuh meddle long
tarruh people bidness.

XXII.

De Cat an de Rat, dem fine one big piece er cheese een er closet. Dem cahr um way fuh share um. Dem cant gree how eh fuh dewide, an dem call een de Fox fuh jedge between um.

De Fox, eh berry cunnin, an eh nebber furgit ehself. Eh bring eh scale, an eh pit de cheese een um. Den eh tek eh knife an eh cut off big piece, an eh pit um one side an eh say dis fuh de jedge. Den eh weigh de cheese gen een de scale, an eh tek um out an eh cut off narrur slice, an eh pit um one side an eh say dat fuh de jedge.

By dis time eh done tek mo ner half de cheese. Wen eh pit de cheese back een de scale, an hole um up gen, Buh Cat an Buh Rat, dem bofe call out: "Hole on, Jedge! Dis ting wrong. You gwine tek all we cheese an leff we none." Buh Fox, him berry bex, on eh gedder de cheese an eh fole up eh scale, an eh holler out: "Begone, you rogue. You lib pon tief, an you gwine tell me how fer do jestice? Good fuh you me only tek de cheese, an leh you go wid you life. Me great mine fuh kill you bofe."

Wid dat, Buh Cat an Buh Rat, dem leff, an Buh Fox, wuh bin de jedge, eat all de cheese.

Wen tief git plunder, better fuh dem fuh share um mongst demself den trus ter call een bigger rogue fur dewide um.

XXIII.

All de animel conjunct togedder fuh buil house an gedder dem winter perwision. Buh Rabbit prommus fuh help, but wen dem call pon um fuh help tote de pole and de bresh, him mek scuse, say him wife berry sick and him bleege fuh tay home an nuss um. All dis bin a lie. Buh Rabbit, him scheemy an lazy. Eh always ready fuh mek big brag bout wuh him gwine do, but eh nebber does come up ter eh wud. Eh hate fuh wuk, an eh lub fuh lib offer tarruh people labuh.

Wen de house done buil, de animel, dem fetch ebry man eh own perwision, an pack um way een eh own place way eh kin git um wen fros fall, an de grass done dead, an de tree done drap eh leaf an eh fruit. De Possum, him bring an pile up pussimmun. De Squirle fetch eh hickry not an eh acorn. De Deer, de Elephant, de Cow, dem gedder an pack way grass an leaf. De Lion and de Tiger an de Wolf an all dem animel wuh lib offer meat, dem ketch dem meat and dry um, an bring um an pit um way een de house. De Bud, dem bring dem seed an

dem wurrum. De Cooter, him hab him corner too, an eh full um long him bittle. Wen
ebry body done gedder eh perwision, dem
shet de do an gone ter dem house fuh ten
ter dem bidness an wait tel winter come,
wen dem gwine lib offer wuh dem bin pit
way. Buh Rabbit, him bin a dodge bout
way nobody kin shum, duh notus wuh
gwine on, an bin a mek eh plan.

Soon es de house full, an de do shet, an
ebry body leff, eh slip een de house an pit
eh yeye on ebry ting, an mek up eh mine fuh
lib topper wuh all dem people bin gedder.
Eh fix one bed fur ehself. Eh gedder water
in piggin an calabash fuh lass um, an den
eh git two oncommon big horn, an eh gone
eenside an fassen up de do, an mek ehself
saterfy. Eh lib day, eh eat, eh sleep, eh pledjur ehself, an eh fine eh bittle right ter eh
han. Dis wuh Buh Rabbit lub. Nuttne mek
um so merry es to lib offer tarruh people.

Fros fall, an de animel biggin fuh tink
bout dem perwision wuh dem bin lay up een
de house. Fus come de Deer, an eh try fuh
open de do fuh git ter him pile er grass.
De do fastne. Buh Deer couldnt mek out
how dat. Eh knock ter de do. Eh knock.
Eh knock. Bimeby Buh Rabbit—wuh bin

56

a yeddy um all de time—tek eh horn, an
eh talk tru um fuh mek er woice big, an eh
say: "Wudduh dat?" Buh Deer, him sorter skittish, an eh faid fuh trus ehself, an
de big woice kinder skade um, but eh mek
out fuh answer: "Duh me, Buh Deer."
Den Buh Rabbit talk tru eh horn: "Wuh
you want yuh, anyhow?" Buh Deer answer: "Me want fuh come een fuh git me
bittle wuh me bin pit way fuh me fuh eat
der winter." Buh Rabbit answer loud tru
eh horn: "You cant come een." Buh Deer
quire: "Who you day eenside?" Den Buh
Rabbit tek eh biggis horn, an eh holler tru
um so loud eh mek de house shake: "Better
man den ebber bin yuh befo."

De woice so sewere Buh Deer skade, an
eh leff, an eh gone tell all dem tarruh animel
say big Sperit gone tek de house way dem
perwision done gedder. De animel stonish,
an dem all conclude fuh go een gang ter de
house an fine out wuh de ting yiz. Wen
dem all gedder, dem tell de Lion—wuh bin
de king beast—fuh quire bout who day
eenside. Buh Lion, him gone ter de do. All
de beastises tan roun fuh yeddy wuh gwine
happne. Buh Lion knock. No answer. Eh
knock gen. No answer. Den eh say: "Who

57

duh dat day een yuh?" Buh Rabbit graff eh big horn, an eh answer back tru um wid all eh strenk: "Better man den ebber bin yuh befo." De woice soun so outlandish, an eh come wid sich er big noise, de beastises all conclude wuh Buh Deer bin tell dem bin so, an dat de Sperit, him bin tek persession er de house. Dem faid fuh bus een de do, an dem all gree fuh leff. Dem did leff, an dem yent fine out tel dis day dat eh been Buh Rabbit wuh fool um, an dat no Sperit bin day none tall.

XXIV

BUH WOLF, BUH RABBIT, AN DE BUTTER.

Buh Wolf, him hire Buh Rabbit fuh help
um wuk eh crap. Eh crap, eh day een de
grass, an Buh Wolf faid eh gwine loss um.
Befo dem state der fiel, Buh Rabbit notus
say Buh Wolf hab een him house er nice
pan er fresh butter. Eh mout water fuh git
some, but eh shame fuh bague Buh Wolf.
Buh Rabbit, him berry lub fuh tief, an eh
mek eh plan fuh git some er dat butter.

Buh Wolf an Buh Rabbit done gone der
fiel an tun een fuh wuk. De sun hot, an
befo long Buh Rabbit biggin fuh drap behine. Den all ob er sutten eh trow down
eh hoe, an eh look way off, an eh cock up eh
yez, an eh holler out: "Me yeddy you. Me
duh comin." Buh Wolf, him tun roun, an eh
say: "Buh Rabbit, wuh you duh do? You
mus be der tun fool. Nobody duh call you."
Buh Rabbit, him mek answer: "Somebody
yiz bin er call me, an me know who dem yiz,
an wuffer dem duh call me. Enty you sabe
me duh preacher? Well, me prommus fuh
bactize er chile dis berry hour, an me mus
go fuh keep me pintment." "Berry well;"
answer Buh Wolf, "dont you loss no time,
fuh dis crap want wuk berry bad."

Buh Rabbit hop off luk eh bin gwine in anarruh direction from dat wuh lead to Buh Wolf house. Wen eh git een de wood, eh slip roun onbeknowinst ter Buh Wolf, an gone een him house an eat hebby outer de pan er butter. Eh wipe eh mouf, an eh sukkle back tell eh git ter de place een de fiel way eh bin leff eh hoe. Eh seem berry merry, an wen Buh Wolf ax um ef he done bactize de chile, eh say yes. Den Buh Wolf ax um wuh dem bin name de chile, an Buh Rabbit tell um say dem bin call um *Fus Biginnin.*

Buh Wolf an Buh Rabbit wuk on. Dem binner hoe tetter. De butter sweeten Buh Rabbit. Him couldnt stop from tink topper um. Eh biggin fuh want mo. De mo eh study bout um de slower eh wuk. Buh Wolf call ter um an tell um fuh hurry. Buh Rabbit mek answer an say eh yiz duh hurry. Bless you soul! een a little while Buh Rabbit, him drap eh hoe an eh holler out: "You right; me bin mose furgit; me comin right off." Buh Wolf, him stonish, an eh say: "Buh Rabbit, you must be loss you sense; who you duh holler teh? Nobody duh call you." Buh Rabbit mek answer: "Somebody yiz bin a call me. Enty you yeddy um?" Buh Wolf say: "No, me no yeddy." Den Buh Rabbit up an tell um say eh hab gagement fur bactize nurrur chile at dis berry hour, an eh mose bin furgit bout um tell eh murrer an eh farruh holler ter um outer de wood an member um. Buh Wolf mek jection gainst Buh Rabbit gwine, but wen Buh Rabbit tell um de chile gwine loss ef eh no git bactize, Buh Wolf lem go. Buh Rabbit do dist iz eh bin done befo. Eh gone een Buh Wolf house, eh tek down de pan gen, an eh eat mona half de butter. Wen eh ketch de fiel, Buh Wolf ax um ef eh done bactize tarruh chile, an eh answer eh yiz. Buh Wolf say: "Duh him duh gal er boy?" Buh Rabbit mek answer say: "Him duh gal." "Wuh eh name?" questun Buh Wolf. *"Half-way,"* answer Buh Rabbit.

Dem wuk on tel de sun biggin fuh lean een de wes. Buh Rabbit still duh study bout dat butter. Eh yent willin fuh go ter eh home an leff any behine. So een de tree hour eh pit eh han up ter eh yez an eh listne. Den eh holler out de turd time, an eh say: "Go on, me duh comin." Buh Wolf ax um. "Way you duh gwine now? Enty you done bactize chillun?" Buh Rabbit tell um eh hab one mo fuh bactize befo sun down, but eh wunt tek um long becase eh lib close by. Den Buh Rabbit slip roun ter Buh Wolf house an clean up de las er de butter. Eh yent leff one grain een de pan.

Wen eh git back Buh Wolf say: "You bactize dat chillun een er hurry; wuh eh name?" Buh Rabbit up an tell um say eh name *Scrapin er de bottom*. Buh Wolf, him nebber bin spicion wuh Buh Rabbit bin up teh. De time come fuh knock off wuk, an wen Buh Wolf want fuh dock Buh Rabbit fuh de time eh loss wen eh bin gone fuh bactize dem tree chillun, Buh Rabbit plead so harde case him bin preacher, dat Buh Wolf, him furgib um an pay um eh full wager. Den eh inwite Buh Rabbit fuh come long um an tek supper wid um. But Buh Rabbit scuse ehself, an light out fer him house, an leff Buh Wolf een de fiel. Buh Rabbit berry scheemy. Eh know say ef eh did bin gone home wid Buh Wolf eh would er see eh track, an fine out who eat eh butter, an dat eh would er lick um.

XXV.

DE EAGLE AN EH CHILLUN.

De Eagle, him duh er wise bud. Eh mek
eh nes on one tall pine tree close de ribber,
er de sea, way nuttne kin git at um. Eh
saterfy wid two chillun. Eh tek good care
er um. Ebry hour eh fetch um snake an
fish, an eh garde um from win an rain an
fowl-hawk, an mek um grow fas. Wen eh
wing kibber wid fedder an eh strong nough
fur fly, wuh Buh Eagle do? Eh wunt leff
dem chillun een de nes fuh lazy an lib pon
topper eh farruh an eh murrer, but eh tek
um on eh wing, an eh sail ober de sea, an eh
tell eh chillun: "De time come fuh you fuh
mek you own libbin. Me feed you long
nough. Now you haffer look out fuh youself." Wid dat, eh fly from onder dem, an
de noung bud, wen eh fine out eh murrer
yent gwine cahr um no furder, an dat dem
haffer shif fuh demself, dem try eh wing an
sail off een de element duh hunt bittle.

People orter tek notus er Buh Eagle an
do jes es him do. Wen you chillun git big
nough fuh wuk, mek um wuk. Dont leh um
set bout de house duh do nuttne, an duh
spek eh farruh an eh murrer fuh fine bittle

an cloze fuh um. Ef you does, you chillun gwine mek you shame, an eh will tun out berry triflin. Eh will keep you dead po, too.

Do same luk Buh Eagle. Mine you chillun well wen dem leetle; an soon es dem big nough fuh wuk, mek um wuk.

XXVI.

CHANTICLEER AN DE BAN-YAD ROOSTER.

You nebber bin see er finer bud den Buh Chanticleer. Eh fedder eh glisten same luk silber een de sun. Eh step so high, an eh yent faid nuttne. Wen eh crow you could yeddy um all tru de settlement. De hen all lub um, an run ter um wenebber him call. Eh can lick all dem tarruh rooster; an jist es soon es eh mek motion at dem, dem run.

Befo eh bin fine um out fuh true, day bin er big yaller Rooster een de gang wuh try fuh spute Buh Chanticleer, an mek eh brag say eh kin lick um. Dem fight. De big yaller Rooster couldnt tan up befo Buh Chanticleer. Eh gaff um, eh pick um een eh back, eh knock um ober, an eh run um out de yad.

Arter dat, de yaller Rooster faid fuh come nigh Buh Chanticleer. Eh run ebry time eh see Buh Chanticleer duh walk towuds um, but eh hab a way fuh debble Buh Chanticleer. Eh go way off, an ebry time eh yeddy Buh Chanticleer flap eh wing an crow, him do de same. Soon a mornin wen Buh Chanticleer crow fuh day, de big yaller

Rooster, him crow too. De ting bodder Buh Chanticleer, an eh want fuh kill um. Eh try hard fuh fine out way eh roose. One day one er de hen wuh blanks ter Buh Chanticleer fambly mek um sensible jist way de yaller Rooster blan roose. Den Buh Chanticleer, him sen fuh Buh Fox. Eh come, an Buh Chanticleer ax um say: "You want one fat Rooster fuh eat?" Buh Fox, him answer: "Yes, me berry glad fuh git um, an heap er tenky ter you too."

Den Buh Chanticleer tell um fuh come de fus moon-shiny night, an him will show um way eh kin git a good supper. Buh Fox happy, an eh prommus fuh come. Eh did come de fus moon-shiny night, an Buh Chanticleer gone long um an pint out de big yaller Rooster duh sleep een one low cedar tree. Buh Fox creep up easy, an graff um an eat um. Wen eh done eat um, an eh duh lick eh mout, Buh Chanticleer ax um: "How you luk um?" Buh Fox mek answer: "Me luk um berry well. Eh bin fat. Eh meat sweet. Me luk um summuch me want mo." Wid dat, an befo Buh Chanticleer kin mek out wuh eh tend fuh do, eh jump pon topper Buh Chanticleer, an mash um ter det, an eat um up.

Wen you want somebody fuh do you sarbis, call pon you fren, but dont trus you eenemy fuh done um.

XXVII.

BUH RABBIT AN DE GROUN-MOLE.

Day nebber bin a man wuh kin equel Buh
Rabbit fuh mek plan fuh lib offer tarruh
people bedout wuk isself. Groun-mole, bin
berry tick. On ebry side dem bin er root
up de tetter patch, and stroy pinder. Nobody know how fuh ketch um, case eh wuk
onder de groun, an wen you go fuh fine um
eh yent dedday.

Buh Rabbit, him see eh chance, an eh tell
ebry body him know how fuh stroy um. De
ting come ter Buh Wolf yez, an eh sen fuh
Buh Rabbit. Buh Rabbit gone ter Buh
Wolf, an eh tell um yes, him hab plan fuh
clear de fiel er Groun-mole, an dat him
wunt charge Buh Wolf nuttne but him
board an lodgment wile him duh ketch an
kill de Groun-mole. Buh Wolf, him say
Buh Rabbit berry kine, an eh gree fuh fine
um. Den Buh Wolf hab one nice bed mek
up fuh Buh Rabbit, an eh tell eh wife fuh
feed um well.

Buh Wolf hab some bidness wuh call um
way from home, an eh spec fuh gone
bout one week. Eh leff Buh Rabbit fuh
clean de Groun-mole outer eh fiel, an den eh

gone. Buh Rabbit, him well saterfy. Ebry mornin, arter brukwus, eh mobe off luk eh bin gwine ter Buh Wolf fiel, an nobody shum tel dinner time. Arter eh done eat er hebby dinner, eh gone gen tel supper time, wen eh come back an eat er hebby supper, an den eh leddown der bed.

Nobody kin see any Groun-mole wuh Buh Rabbit der ketch, but eh tell Buh Wolf wife dat eh bin er kill heap er dem ebry day, an dat eh gwine soon clear de fiel. De ting gone on dis way tel Buh Wolf tun home. Wen eh retch eh house eh quire bout Buh Rabbit, an eh wife tell um wuh Buh Rabbit bin er say an er do, an dat Buh Rabbit gone der fiel dist arter brukwus. Buh Wolf say him gwine see fuh ehself wuh Buh Rabbit duh do, an wuh plan eh fix fuh ketch de Groun-mole.

Wen eh git der fiel eh look up an down, an eh yent see no sign er Buh Rabbit. Eh notus eh crap, an de Groun-mole duh eat um wus den nebber. Eh sarche fuh Buh Rabbit track, an eh cant shum no way. Buh Wolf mek up eh mine dat Buh Rabbit yent do de fus ting een de fiel. De sun hot. Buh Wolf gone een de edge er de wood, an day eh come pon topper Buh Rabbit tretch

out een er bed wuh eh bin mek outer pine
straw onder one tree, fas tersleep. Eh yent
bin study bout Buh Wolf, er de Groun-mole
wuh bin er bodder de fiel. Buh Wolf slip
up, an eh graff um tight. Buh Rabbit so
skade eh furgit fuh lie, an Buh Wolf mek
um confess eh yent know how fuh ketch
Groun-mole, dat eh nebber did kill none, an
dat eh bin lib offer Buh Wolf bittle ebber
sence eh leff.

Buh Wolf, him so bex eh git grape wine an
eh tie Buh Rabbit han an foot, an eh lick um
tel eh tired. All dis time Buh Rabbit bin
eh holler an er bague. At lenk Buh Wolf
loose um, an run um offer de place.

Eh yent offen Buh Rabbit ketch at him
trick, but eh meet eh match dis time.

XXVIII.

BUH RABBIT AN DE ROCK-SOUP.

Anurrer way Buh Rabbit hab fuh mek eh
libbin bedout wuk bin dis. Eh hab een eh
pocket er pooty, smoode rock, bout de size
ob er tukrey agg. Wid dem people wuh no
quaintun wid um eh pass ehself off fuh er
fus-class cook, an eh tell um say eh hab one
rock wuh mek pruppus fuh gie soup de bes
tase; an dat de soup wuh mek long dat
rock sweeter den all edder soup.

Eh gone ter Buh Bear house, an Buh
Bear hearky ter um, an gage um fuh mek
some soup long eh rock. Buh Rabbit pit on
de pot, an eh bile water een um long de
stone. Den eh call fuh meat, an wegetable,
an all kind er seaznin, an eh stir um an eh
cook um all togerrur, an eh did mek er nice
soup. Eh fool Buh Bear, an eh mek um
bliebe say eh bin de rock wuh gib sich er
rich flaber ter de soup, wen de fac bin say
de rock yent hab nuttne fuh do long um, but
de tarruh ting wuh gone een de pot, dem
duh de ting wuh mek de soup. Buh Rabbit
git big dinner at Buh Bear house dat day.

Anurrer time, wen eh bin berry hongry,
eh gone ter Buh Cooter house, an eh fool um

same fashion, an eh git er hebby dinner day too.

Eh do dis way fuh some time, guine from house teh house.

At lenk eh miss an gone ter Buh Fox house, an tell um bout eh rock-soup. Buh Fox, him no fool. Him duh er smate man, an eh see tru de ting right off. But eh yent leh Buh Rabbit see dat eh spicion anyting, an eh tell um fuh go head an mek eh soup. Eh han out wuhebber Buh Rabbit call fuh, an eh wait topper um tel de soup done. Den eh tase um, an wen eh fine eh tase same luk any edder soup mek long de ting wuh eh han Buh Rabbit fuh pit een de pot, eh tek Buh Rabbit rock, an eh trow um down de well, an eh cuss Buh Rabbit fur er swindler, an mek um shame befo all eh fambly, an mek um leff.

Buh Rabbit an Buh Fox, bofe er dem berry cunnin, but dis time Buh Fox him cunnin moner Buh Rabbit.

XXIX.

Two fren, dem bin a mek one journey togerruh. Dem haffer go tru one tick swamp
wuh full er bear an edder warmint. Dem
prommus fuh tan ter one anurrer, an help
one anurrer out ef de warmint should tack
dem. Dem yent bin git half way tru de
swamp wen one big black Bear jump outer
de bush an mek fur dem. Steader one er
dem tan fur help fight um, eh leff eh fren
an clime one tree. De tarruh fren bin yeddy
say Bear no gwine eat dead people, so him
leddown on de groun, an hole eh bref, an
shet eh yeye, an mek out say him bin dead.
De Bear come up ter um, an smell um, an
tun um ober, an try fuh ketch eh bref.
Wen eh fine eh cant ketch eh bref, eh gone
off leely way an eh watch um. Den eh tun
back an smell um gen, an notus um close.
At lenk eh mek up eh mine say de man bin
dead fuh true; an wid dat eh leff um fuh
good an gone back der wood. All dis time
de tarruh fren duh squinch ehself up een de
tree duh watch wuh bin gwine on. Eh dat
skade eh wunt do nuttne fuh help eh fren,
er try fuh run de Bear off.

Wen eh fine de Bear done gone fuh sho, eh holler ter him fren say: "Wuh de Bear bin tell you? Him an you seem luk you bin hab close combersation." Den eh fren mek answer: "Eh bin tell me nebber fuh trus nobody wuh call ehself fren, an wuh gwine run luk er coward soon es trouble come."

XXX.

One Ole Man bin berry tired long wuk.
Him want fuh stop an tek eh pledjur all day
een him house. Eh bex long de Buckra
wuh gie um task, an mek um ten ter um.
Eh constant duh pray, so people kin yeddy
um, dat Det would come an cahr way eh
Mossa, an eh Mistis, an de Obersheer. De
Obersheer him yeddy wuh de Ole Man bin
a pray fuh, an eh tell de Mossa, an dem fix
plan fuh hab fun long de Ole Man. Wen
night come, an ebryting on de plantation
done gone bed, de Mossa, him tek one long
white gown wuh ketch down ter eh foot, an
eh pit um on, an eh gone ter de Ole Man
house. Eh push de do open, an day bin de
Ole Man duh siddown on eh bench duh nod
by de fire. De Ole Man yeddy say some
body come ter him do, an wen eh tun roun
fuh look, eh see one tall somebody all wrop
up head an yez een white. Eh git skade,
an tink duh Sperit. Eh quire: "Who duh
dat?" De Sperit, wuh bin de Mossa dress
up een de white gown wuh kibber um all
ober, mek answer way down een him troat:
"Duh me, Det, wuh you bin a pray fuh."

Den de Ole Man say: "You come fuh
Mossa?" De Sperit shake eh head. Eh
say gen: "You come fuh Mistis?" De
Sperit shake eh head gen. De Ole Man
quire gen: "Den you musser come fuh de
Obersheer?" De Sperit shake eh head gen.
De Ole Man rale skade now, an eh study fuh
leely while, an den eh questun gen: "Ef
you no come fuh Mossa, ner Mistis, ner de
Obersheer, who de Debble you come fuh?"
Den de Sperit, eh bow eh head low an eh
mek answer: "Me come fuh you." De Ole
Man hair rise. Eh git up. Eh bus tru de
back do. Eh run tru de gaden, an eh mek
fuh de wood. Nobody yent shum tel arter
brukwus next mornin, an den eh tell ebry
body say Det bin come fur um last night,
but dat him bin dodge um. Arter dat nobody ebber yeddy um mek no mo prayer
bout Det.

XXXI

DE KING AN EH RING.

One time dere was a King wuh bin done
git marry, an eh bin hab one fine Ring wuh
him bin call eh gagement Ring. Dat King,
him bin hab tree serbant wuh wait bout him
table, an clean him shoes, an do wuhebber
him want um fuh do. Dem bin tek tun
een clean de shoes. One clean um one
mornin, anurrur one clean um nex mornin,
an de edder one clean um de nex. One er
dem serbant tief de King Ring. De King
try fuh fine out which one er de tree bin tek
um, an eh fail. Dem wunt tell topper one
anurrur, an de ting bodder de King berry
bad. Eh faid say ef eh cant git back eh
gagement Ring all eh good luck gwine leff
um. Eh call een eh fren an wise man fuh
help um pint out de tief an fine dat Ring, an
dem cant.

One day de King notus er strange man
duh walk bout him gaden, an eh sen an hab
um brung ter um. Wen eh questun um, de
man tell um say him bin a po man, an dat
eh mek eh libbin by cunjur. De King tell
um eh bin dis de man eh duh hunt fur, an
eh want um fuh fine eh Ring. Eh mek um

quaintun bout wen de Ring tuk, an who eh tink tief um; an eh say eh gwine gie um fibe day time fuh pint out de man wuh bin tek de Ring, an mek um tun um. Mo na dat, eh prommus um big money ef eh git back de Ring widin de fibe day; but eh treaten um fuh kill um ef eh fail fuh fine um eenside dat time. Eh charge eh serbant fuh tek good care er de conjur man, an feed um high.

De rale name er dis cunjur man bin *Robin,* but him yent bin gib dis name ter de King.

De cunjur man try fuh fine out de tief, but eh miss. Four day gone, an de Ring yent fine. De cunjur man, him berry sad, an eh faid say eh gwine fail, an de King gwine tek eh head off.

De mornin ob de fibe day de King git up soon, an pledjur ehself by tek er walk een eh gaden. Wile eh duh tan onder one berry tree, one robin-red-bres, wuh bin er eat de berry, choke an fall der groun. De King pick um up, an eh dead in eh han. Den eh tek um, an wrop um up een eh henkerchef, an pit um een eh hat. Eh sen fuh de cunjur man, an eh tell um eh time mose out, an dat ef eh no fine de Ring by sundown eh gwine

kill um. Eh say ter um, mooōber, dat eh
doubt um, an dat eh yent bliebe eh kin cunjur none tall; dat ef eh kin cunjur eh mus
tell um right off wuh eh got een him hat.
De cunjur man so skade eh yent say nuttne
cept pity ehself, an say: "Po Robin! Po
Robin!" De King tek um say eh bin mean
de bud, an eh confidance rise, an eh mek answer: "You right, me yiz hab one robin een
me hat; an becase you tell true, me gwine
gie you six day mo fuh fine out who tief de
Ring." De cunjur man rale glad, an de ting
mek de King an all eh fren an de serbant
bliebe say eh kin cunjur fur true. De tree
serbant wuh bin een cohoot fuh tief de Ring,
an wuh bin know all bout um, biggin fuh
faid say dem bin gwine fuh git fine out.

De nex mornin, wen one er dem serbant
come down wid de King shoes, de cunjur
man pint eh finger at um an eh say: "You
duh one er de tief." De man look condemn,
but eh mek answer, say: "Him yent." De
nex mornin wen de tarrur serbant fetch de
King shoes down fuh clean um, de cunjur
man pint him finger at um an eh say: "You
duh nudder one er dem tief." De man rale
skade, but eh schway say him yent know
nuttne bout de Ring. De nex mornin wen de

edder serbant duh clean de King shoes, de cunjur man gone up ter um an pint eh finger right een eh face, an eh say: "You duh de tird man wuh know bout dis Ring an help fuh tief um." De man yeye fall, but him wouldnt confess.

Dat same ebenin all tree dem serbant, dem come ter de cunjur man an fetch de Ring, an confess say dem been tek um, an dem bague de cunjur man fuh fix plan fuh clear dem. Him so glad him git de Ring him prommus fuh do dist as dem say. So eh tell dem fuh fetch one big tukrey-gobbler ter um. Dem gone an ketch de biggis een de gang, an brung um ter de cunjur man. Eh tek de Ring an eh mix um long corn-flour, an eh poke em een de tukrey-gobbler craw. Den eh mark de bud so him kin know um gen, an eh tun um loose.

De cunjur man, him gone right off ter de King, an eh tell um say him kin pint out way de Ring day. De King, him berry glad, an eh collec all him fren fuh see de cunjur man pint out de Ring. Wen dem all gedder, de conjur man, him ax de King fuh hab all him tukrey dribe befo um. De King him do so, an as de tukrey bin er walk pass, de conjur man pint out one big tukrey-gobbler an tell de King say him hab de Ring een him craw. Wid dat, de King mek one er him serbant ketch de gobbler an rip open eh craw, an day, sho nuff, was de Ring. De King, him bin so rejoice eh gib high praise ter de cunjur man, an eh gie um big money, an mek um rich. De tree serbant too, wuh bin de tief, dem so happy cause de cunjur man yent spose dem ter de King dat dem mek present ter um too, an bin eh fren all dem life.

XXXII.

BUH LION, BUH RABBIT, BUH FOX, AN BUH ROCCOON.

Buh Lion, him bin keep er bank. Een dat bank him hab chicken, en hog, en sheep. Buh Fox, him marry ter Buh Coon darter. Buh Fox farruh-een-law, him bin er rogue. Buh Coon an Buh Rabbit mek er plan fuh rob Buh Lion bank, an dem usen fuh tek ting outer um ebry now en den, an nobody kin fine out who duh de tief. Buh Fox, Buh Rabbit, an Buh Coon, dem day fas fren, an dem constant keep compny. Buh Rabbit him tell Buh Lion, say him know de man wuh duh rob him bank, but eh yent want talk eh name, an eh vise Buh Lion fuh set steel trap fuh ketch de tief. Buh Lion do es him say, an de nex night, wen Buh Coon, Buh Fox, an Buh Rabbit gone fuh rob de bank gen, Buh Coon, him walk topper de trap an eh ketch um by eh foot. De ting broke Buh Coon leg, an eh hot um berry bad, but eh faid fuh holler, case, ef eh did holler, eh know Buh Lion gwine run day an kill um. So eh leddown an moan, an beg eh fren fuh help um. Buh Fox an Buh Rabbit, dem study ober de ting, an

82

dem mek up dem mine say ef Buh Lion
fine Buh Coon een de trap, eh not only
gwine kill Buh Coon, but eh will sen an kill
all eh fambly. Den dem conclude dat de
bes ting fuh do bin dat Buh Fox—wuh
bin him son-een-law—mus tek one swode
an chop Buh Coon head off an bury um, an
dat eh skin Buh Coon an bury eh hide an
eh cloze, an leff Buh Coon nekked een de
trap, so nobody kin tell who bin ketch.

Buh Fox, him do es dem gree. De nex
mornin wen Buh Lion zamine eh trap, eh
fine de tief done ketch. Eh call een eh fren
fuh consult, but es de body done strip, an
eh head done cut off an gone, nobody could
mek up eh mine who de tief bin. Buh Lion,
him say him gwine fine out who de tief yiz,
an who de man wuh cut eh head off an skin
um.

Buh Rabbit, him come up bout dis time,
an him swade Buh Lion fuh sen fuh one
cart, an pit de dead body een um, an leh one
er eh han heng ober one side er de cart, an
gedder him soldier an pit one gang on de
leff han side an de tarruh gang on de right
han side, an mek de music go befo, an leh
dem all march down de middle er de street
een Buh Lion town all de lenk er de street;

83

an ef de soldier yeddy anybody duh scream an duh cry een any one er de house, den de soldier mus go ter dat house an kill ebry body wuh lib day, case dat mus be de fambly er de tief. Buh Lion, him well please, an him gie order, an hab de ting done jes es Buh Rabbit bin plan.

Wen de compny bin er march wid de dead body er de tief een de cart, jes es dem come befo de do er de house way Buh Fox lib, wuh bin marry Buh Roccoon darter, him wife bin er look outer de winder, an eh see eh pa han duh heng ober de side er de cart, an eh know um, an eh holler an scream an fall down an faint way. Den de soldier wuh bin on de right han side er de cart, dem run ter de house way dem yeddy de screamin an de hollerin, an dem bus een de do an gone een fuh kill de whole fambly. Buh Fox, wen eh see wuh happne, tek one knife an eh cut off one er him finger, an eh run to de do, an eh meet de soldier, an eh show um eh han der bleed, an eh tell um say eh bin dis loose one er eh finger, an eh wife dat scade wen eh see wuh happne ter um, dat eh holler an faint way. So Buh Fox fool de soldier, an dem gone back an jine de compny an march on. Dat night dem camp een de en er de street, an halfer de soldier bin on one side de cart, an tarruh half bin on tarruh side duh guade de body er de tief wuh head cut off.

Wen Buh Fox wife come teh, eh spicion say Buh Fox bin know who kill eh pa,— wuh bin Buh Roccoon,—an eh tell eh husbun, Buh Fox, say ef eh dont git eh pa body an bring um ter um dat berry night, eh gwine tell Buh Lion him bliebe de one wuh cut eh farruh—Buh Coon—head off an hide um, duh eh own husbun,—Buh Fox. Buh Fox tell um say him yent know nuttne bout de ting, an eh try fuh swade um no fuh go nigh Buh Lion. Wen eh fine eh wife mine done mek up, an no way fuh him fuh git out cept fuh fetch Buh Coon body ter eh wife, eh gone ter Buh Rabbit fuh vise um an fuh help um. Buh Rabbit, him yeddy all wuh Buh Fox hab fuh say, an den eh say: "Me tell you wuh you do. To-night gwine cole. Dem soldier duh camp der street, an dem yent hab no fire. Dem berry lub rum. Bout middle night you tek you horse an you paint one side er um white, an de tarruh side er um black. You cahr two jug er rum, an you ride ter de camp, an you gie one jug ter de gang er soldier

wuh day on de right, an de edder jug ter
de tarruh gang wuh day on de leff, an wen
dem drunk you kin tek Buh Coon body
outer de cart an cahr um home."

Buh Fox, him wrop him head an yez up
so nobody kin know um, an eh paint eh horse
one side white an tarruh side black, an eh tek
eh two jug er rum an eh ride ter de camp,
an eh do dis es Buh Rabbit bin tell um fuh
do. De soldier, dem berry glad fuh git de
rum. Dem tink two man fetch um,—one
duh ride er white horse, an de edder duh
ride er black horse. Dem drink tell dem
drunk, an den Buh Fox slip way wid Buh
Coon body ter eh wife house, an him an eh
wife bury um een de gaden same night onbeknowinst ter ebry body.

De nex mornin wen de soldier wake up,
de cart day day, but de body done gone.
De soldier wuh camp on de leff, dem say de
man wuh ride on er white horse mus er tief
um; an de soldier wuh camp on de right,
dem say de man wuh ride on er black horse
him mus er tief um. So Buh Fox cuhfuse
dem two gang er soldier, an dem nebber did
fine um out.

Buh Rabbit, him scheemy mona all dem
tarruh cretur. Him do all dis, an yet him

stay fren wid Buh Lion, Buh Fox, an wid
Buh Coon fambly.

XXXIII.

BUH RABBIT, BUH WOLF, AN DE PORPUS.

Ebber sence dat time wen Buh Wolf
ketch Buh Rabbit duh tief water outer him
spring, an eh bin tie um ter de spakleberry
bush an lick um, Buh Rabbit hate Buh
Wolf an mek plan fuh git eben wid um.

Dem all two lub fish. Buh Rabbit an
Buh Porpus bin good fren, an many er time
Buh Porpus blan gie Buh Rabbit some er
de fish wuh him der ketch. One day, Buh
Porpus, him bin berry lucky een eh fishin,
an eh fetch fuh Buh Rabbit mo ner two
quart er gannet mullet, and blow um on de
bank way Buh Rabbit kin git um dout wet
eh foot. Buh Rabbit, him tell um heap er
tenky, an eh cahr um ter him house. Befo
eh part compny wid Buh Porpus, eh tell um
how Buh Wolf bin ketch um an tie um an
lick um, how eh bex long Buh Wolf, an how
eh want Buh Porpus fuh help um fuh punish
Buh Wolf. Den dem mek plan lucker dis:
Buh Porpus bin fuh come back ter de same
place nex day an leh Buh Rabbit tie grape-
wine roun um, so Buh Wolf kin pull um
outer de water fuh eat um. Wen Buh
Wolf tek eh holt fuh pull Buh Porpus

outer de water, den Buh Porpus wus teh mek eh flut an juk Buh Wolf een de ribber an drown um. So dey gree, an Buh Rabbit gone home long eh fish.

Wen eh git ter eh house eh sen one er him gal to Buh Wolf house fuh tell um him hab some nice fish, an ter eenwite Buh Wolf an him fambly fuh tek brukwus long um nex mornin. Buh Wolf, him well please, an eh say him an eh fambly gwine come wid pled-jur.

Dem did come. De fish sweet. Buh Wolf, him an eh wife an eh chillun joy um berry much. Buh Wolf ax Buh Rabbit way eh git de fish, an Buh Rabbit tell um say him fren, Buh Porpus, blan ketch um fur um, an dat him hab er pintment dat berry day wid Buh Porpus. Buh Wolf bague Buh Rabbit fuh leh him go long too, an see ef him couldnt mek rangement wid Buh Porpus fuh fine him een fish. Buh Rabbit say him willin; so dem finish brukwus an gone fuh meet Buh Porpus.

Es dem duh gwine Buh Rabbit tell Buh Wolf say Porpus meat berry nice, an eh tink mebbe dem kin ketch Buh Porpus an eat um. Buh Wolf quire: "How you gwine do um?" Den Buh Rabbit, him mek answer: "Me tell you how we gwine wuk dis ting. Me good fren ter Buh Porpus, an wen we git ter de ribber bank me gwine tell Buh Porpus leh we hab er game, an see who kin pull de strongis. Den we will tek er grape-wine an tie um roun Buh Porpus head, an you an me will tek turrer een, an we sholy kin drag Buh Porpus outer de ribber; an wen we git um out eh gwine dead, an we will hab heap er bittle fuh eat." Buh Wolf, him no bin know de plan wuh Buh Rabbit aready done fix wid Buh Porpus, an so eh gree ter all wuh Buh Rabbit bin say.

Wen dem git ter de ribber bank, day was Buh Porpus duh wait fur Buh Rabbit. Buh Rabbit mek um quaintum wid Buh Wolf, an arter er while Buh Wolf ax Buh Porpus fuh fine um een fish same luk eh fine Buh Rabbit, an Buh Porpus gree fur do so. Den Buh Rabbit, him say: "Leh we hab some fun, an see who kin pull de strongis: Buh Porpus genst me an Buh Wolf." Buh Porpus say him willin. Wid dat, Buh Rabbit git one long grape-wine, an eh tie one een roun Buh Porpus head, an de tarruh een eh tie fus roun Buh Wolf body, an den roun him own; but eh leff de een loose, so him kin slip out. Den eh gie de wud fuh pull.

Es eh done dat eh slip outer de wine, an leff Buh Wolf lone fuh pull genst Buh Porpus. At de fus, wen Buh Porpus ease isself off een de ribber, eh pull sorter light, an den eh gie way, and Buh Wolf, him tought him gwine outpull um. But een er leely while Buh Porpus sorter hump eh back an flut eh tail, an yuh Buh Wolf come fuh de water. Eh dig eh paw een de san, an eh holler ter Buh Rabbit fuh tun um loose; but Buh Rabbit wouldnt tetch um, an so Buh Porpus drag um, duh scuffle an duh holler, clean een de ribber an onder de water, an drown Buh Wolf. Arter dat Buh Porpus swim back ter de bank an Buh Rabbit tek off de grape-wine from roun eh neck, an dem leff Buh Wolf een de water fuh shark an alligatur fuh eat.

Buh Rabbit an Buh Porpus done Buh Wolf er mean trick.

XXXIV.

DE DEBBLE AN MAY BELLE.

De Debble, him kin tek all sorter shape
fuh cahr out him plan an fool people. Sometime eh mek isself inter wolf fuh kill you
sheep. Narruh time eh tek de shape er alligatur fuh worry you duck an goose. Den
eh look lucker white deer, an eh fly tru de
wood, dout mek no noise, fuh skade people
duh walk long de big road. Den eh come
same lucker owl, an eh holler down you
chimbly an eh tarrify ebry body wen dem
duh tun flour een de pot. Den wen you
sick, eh gone eensider you lucker a wurrum,
an eh gie you all sorter misry. Den gen,
eh kin tek de shape er man, en pass isself
off fur great gentleman long de lady. Day
yent nuttne wuh de Debble cant do ef eh
mek up eh mine ter um.

One time day was a berry pooty noung
ooman name May Belle. Him farruh bin
rich, an eh dress um up ter de notch, an eh
gie um saddle horse fuh ride, an carriage
fuh dribe, an plenty er serbant fuh wait on
um, an ebry good bittle fuh eat, an rockin-
chair fuh set een, an orgin fuh play topper.

All de noung man een de county bin er cote um an er try fuh marry um.

One day one strange man come fuh wisit um. Eh dress up better ner all dem tarruh gentlemans. Eh hab on new beber hat, wuh shine lucker glass, an eh hab side whisker comb so nice, an glub on eh han, an new cloze, an eh dribe up een er fine carriage wid four horse, an de driber hab er keen lash wuh pop so clear you could yeddy um way down de road.

De noung lady tek wid um right off. Eh hab sich er good manners, an eh talk so perlite, an eh ack so rich, ebry body gie way ter um, an eh outshine all dem tarruh Buckra wuh bin er cote de gal, an eh marry um befo de week out, an eh tek um een eh carriage, an eh dribe um off ter him house. Dat house bin een er deestant part er de country, buil on er hill. Nobody bin lib close. Eh bin de fines house een de whole settlement. Eh hab piazza all roun an roun, an eenside ebry ting look berry nice an pooty.

Wen dem dribe up ter de step, de Debble, wuh bin de husbun, han eh Bride een de pahler, an set um een one rockin-chair, an tell um de whole house blanks ter um, an eh mus mek isself saterfy an joy isself.

93

Ebry ting gone long berry well fur some time, an de noung wife hab ebry ting him call fur. One mornin, wen eh husbun leff de house fur ten ter eh bidness, an eh wife bin er ramble bout de room, eh fine one key duh heng up by isself. Eh wonder wuh key dat, an wuh do eh open. Eh tek um an eh try one lock arter anurrer, but de key wunt fit. Bimeby eh gone duh garret, an eh see one do up day wuh bin lock. Eh pit de key ter de hole an eh onlock de do, an wen eh open um lo! an behole! eh see een de closet tree noung ooman duh heng up long dem neck, an dem bin all dead. De ting skade de gal so bad eh scacely hab han fuh shet de do an lock um gen. But arter a while eh manage fuh do dat, an den eh mek hase an heng de key way eh bin fine um. De Bride faid fuh ax eh husbun bout de ting. All eh joy done gone. Eh want fuh git way, but him dunno how fuh do um. Eh yent hab nobody fuh truss fuh sen ter eh farruh an bredder fuh come an tek um way.

Eh husbun bin gen um one nice ridin horse fuh tek eh pledjur long ebry mornin an ebenin. De Debble so busy eh wife haffer ride by isself. De po gal yent say nuttne ter nobody bout wuh eh see een de

closet der garret. Eh hide eh feelin, but eh
berry onsaterfy een eh mine.

De nex mornin, wen eh bin er tek eh ride,
soon es eh git outer yearin, eh biggin fuh
cry, an fuh pity isself, an say eh wish eh bin
back ter eh farruh house, an talk eh mine
dat eh faid eh husbun, wen eh git tired long
um, gwine kill um an heng um long de tarruh ooman wuh day een de closet duh garret.
Him no know de horse wuh him duh ride
bin a yeddy um, an duh notus wuh him duh
say. All ob er sutten de horse open eh
mout, an eh ax eh missis: "Enty you know
who you marry ter? You husbun duh de
Debble, an wen eh saterfy long you eh gwine
bex wid you an kill you same luk eh done
kill dem tarruh wife wuh eh bin hab befo eh
bring you yuh." De po ooman dat skade
eh ready fuh fall off. Eh mose faint way.
Eh heart duh flutter een eh bres. All eh
strenk gie way. Eh cry. Eh gib up fuh
loss. Den eh bague de horse fuh pity um,
an help um, an tek um back ter him fambly.
De horse sorry fur um, an eh prommus fuh
try an sabe um, but eh tell um fuh keep eh
mout shet, an mek no rackit bout de ting.
Mo na dat, eh tell um, de nex mornin wen
eh come fuh ride, eh mus fetch een eh pocket

95

four big nail wuh day on de mantlepiece een de Debble room, an dem will help um fuh git way.

De po ooman tenk um berry much, an dem gone back an nobody bin know bout dis plan. De nex mornin wen de Debble, wuh bin him husbun, leff de house an gone fuh mine eh bidness, eh wife fine de nail dis es de horse bin say, an eh pit um een eh pocket. Den eh call fuh him ridin horse same luk eh ebber done, an eh gone down de road fuh ride. Soon es eh git outer de sight er de house, de good horse eh men eh pace; an, befo de middle er de day, eh tell eh missis fuh drap one er dem nail een de road. Eh missis did drap um, an right off one big bank er san riz up clean cross de road, so nobody could dribe ober. Wen night come on dem drap anurrur nail, middle night anurrer, an es de sun duh rise dem drap de las one. Ebry time de nail drap, de big bank er san rise up an shet up de road. De horse run so fas eh retch de ooman farruh house by brukwus time een de mornin. Eh fambly stonish fuh see um, an wen eh tell dem wuh mek eh come back, eh farruh an eh bredder git dem gun fur shoot de Debble ef eh come fuh tek de gal back.

Wen de Debble fine out say eh wife yent
come back from ride, eh biggin fuh spicion
someting; an arter dinner eh git een eh
carriage fuh hunt eh wife. Eh tek de big
road, an eh mek eh driber pit de lick ter de
horse, but eh cant see ner yeddy nuttne bout
eh wife. Bimeby eh come pon topper de fus
bank er san een de road, an den him bin
know right off wuh happne. Eh mek eh
horse grabble tru, an den eh dribe straight
fur eh farruh-een-law house. Eh blow eh
hot bref behine eh horse, an eh mek um run
lucker de win. Eh haffer stop fuh git tru
dem tarruh bank er san wuh de edder nail
bin mek, an so eh loss eh time an nebber
did obertek eh wife. Wen eh tun een de
abnue wuh lead ter eh wife farruh house, eh
see eh wife an all eh fambly day een de
piazza duh watch de road. Eh farruh-een-
law an eh bredder-een-law hab gun een dem
han. De Debble, him no faid gun, an eh
dribe right up, an eh ax eh wife wuh mek
um run way. Befo eh kin answer, eh tell
um fuh git right een de carriage an go back
home long um. Eh wife say eh wunt, an eh
hole on ter eh farruh. Den de Debble git
berry bex an schway say him gwine cahr um
any how. Wid dat, eh light outer de car-

riage an mek fuh de piazza fuh graff eh
wife. Eh farruh an eh bredder tell um fuh
tan back an leh de gal lone. De Debble
wunt yeddy dem, an es eh rise de step de
farruh an de bredder er de noung ooman
shoot de Debble long buck-shot. De shot
drap offer um dout hot um, an eh come
right on. Dist es eh bin guine tek de gal
eh change eh mine, an eh tun ter eh old self,
wid eh forky tail, an eh claw, an eh bat-
wing, an eh owl yez, an eh blow fire outer eh
mout, an eh bun up eh wife, an him farruh,
an him murrer, an him bredder, an de house,
an ebry ting wuh day een um. Not a ting
leff fuh show way de house bin. Eh bun
up de horse too wuh bin help eh wife fuh
run way. Den eh change back ter de shape
er a man dist es befo, an eh git een him carriage, an eh dribe back ter him house same
luk nuttne bin happne.

"De Debble," added Daddy Cudjo, as he
concluded this story, "duh de wus ting een
dis wul an de nex. Me nebber gwine hab
nuttne fuh do long um. Me faid um wus
den rattlesnake; an dat ting wuh dem call
Hell, me nebber wan shum ner go nigh um."

XXXV.

DE OLE MAN AN DE COON.

One time er rich Buckra hab er senserble ole man serbant wuh come from Afreka. Dis ole nigger bin know ebryting bout ebryting. Nobody could tun um wid questun. Eh Mossa try um heap er time, an eh ebber did mek right answer. Eh fren try um too, an dem nebber ketch um duh miss. De Buckra brag heaby on de ole man, an berry offne eh win bet topper um. One day de Buckra man gen er big dinner, an eh een-wite heaper fren ter him house. Eh lay er wager say nobody kin ax eh ole serbant er questun wuh him couldnt answer, an eh gie eh fren lief fuh try de ole man any fashion dem want. De money pit up, an de fren call one boy, wuh bin er wuk bout de lot, an dem sen um der wood fuh ketch one coon. De boy gone wid eh dog. Wen dinner done ober, an de gentlemans duh set een de piazza duh talk, de boy come back wid er roccoon. Dem call fuh er barrel, an dem tek de coon an pit um een an head um up complete, so nobody kin see wuh day eenside.

Den dem sen fuh de ole Afreka nigger. Eh bin er hoe cotton der fiel, an nobody

bin tell um wuh mek dem sen fuh um. Eh
come; an den eh Mossa say: "Ole man, we
sen fuh you fuh tell we wuh day een dis barrel." De ole man look at um, an walk roun
um, an notus um close, an listne fuh see ef
eh could yeddy anyting duh mobe. All de
gentlemans duh watch um. Wen de ole man
mek up eh mine eh couldnt fine out wuh day
een de barrel, eh stop, eh study, eh cratch
eh head, an den eh mek answer: "Mossa,
hoona done head de ole coon dis time."

Eh no bin know say him bin er speak er
true wud bout wuh bin een de barrel. Eh
bin er talk bout ehself wen eh say dem bin
head de ole coon dis time, but eh Mossa an
de tarruh gentlemans no know, and dem all
gie de ole man big praise. Eh Mossa win de
bet, an eh share de silber money wid de ole
man.

XXXVI.

BUH RABBIT AN DE CRAWFISH.

Arter Buh Wolf bin lick Buh Rabbit an trow um een de brier patch case eh ketch um der tief water outer him spring, Buh Rabbit faid fuh meet Buh Wolf, an him leff an gone buil ehself new house een Buh Bear settlement. Buh Bear, him hab well, an steader Buh Rabbit fine him own water, eh blan slip ter Buh Bear well an tief water outer um. Buh Bear fine dis out, but Buh Rabbit so scheemy Buh Bear couldnt pit eh han topper um fuh ketch um. So eh git one big crawfish an eh pit um een de well, an eh tell um fuh gard de well, an fastne ebrybody wuh come day fuh tief water.

De nex time Buh Rabbit gone der well long him calabash fuh git some water, de fus ting eh know de crawfish grab um by eh tail. Buh Rabbit holler, an een eh pull way eh leff eh tail een de crawfish claw. An dat de way Buh Rabbit come fuh loss eh tail. Eh tail stumpy tel dis day.

XXXVII.

BUH RABBIT AN BUH ELEPHUNT.

You ebber notus say Buh Elephunt yez all de time duh heng down, an eh cant cock um up luk de tarruh creetuh? Eh hinge to eh yez look luk eh broke. You know wuh mek so? Ef you yent know, lemme tell you.

Buh Rabbit an Buh Elephunt, dem blan ramble tru de same wood. Buh Rabbit, him lib offer de noung grass, an Buh Elephunt, him eat de tree limb. Dem bin quaintun wid one anurrur; an, weneber dem meet, dem nusen fuh pass de time er day. Buh Rabbit, him too leetle fuh Buh Elephunt fuh keep compny long.

Een de spring er de year Buh Rabbit bin mek eh nes onder one bush, an eh line um an eh kibber um ober complete long sofe dry grass. Eh hab tree leely chillun een dat nes. One day Buh Elephunt bin er hunt eh bittle, an eh gone miss an mash topper Buh Rabbit nes, an kill eh chillun. Buh Rabbit no bin day at de time, an wen eh git back eh fine eh nes done broke up, an all tree eh chillun squash flat. Eh see by de track say Buh Elephunt bin do dat. Eh

gone right off an eh tackle Buh Elephunt
bout um. Buh Elephunt mek answer an say
him yent do um; him yent know nuttne
bout um. Wen Buh Rabbit fine eh cant
git no saterfaction outer Buh Elephant, eh
cut down, an eh berry bex, an eh mek plan
fuh git eeben wid Buh Elephunt fuh de
big damage wuh him bin done ter um an
eh fambly.

Eh quaintun wid de place way Buh Elephunt blan leddown fuh tek eh res; so eh
watch um, an wen eh done gone der bed, Buh
Rabbit, him slip back an eh call eh wife,
and dem gedder dry leaf an dead grass, an
dem tote um ter de spot way Buh Elephunt
duh sleep, an dem full all two Buh Elephunt yez long de leaf an grass. Den dem
trike fire an clap um ter de dry grass an
leaf wuh dem bin pit een Buh Elephunt yez.
Eh blaze up. Buh Elephunt wake. Eh
couldnt mek out wuh happne. De ting biggin fuh bun um bad. Eh holler fuh somebody fuh help um. Eh roll ober an try fuh
out de fire een eh yez. Eh tek eh trunk an
try fuh lick um out, but befo de fire done
out, eh bun de hinge er all two eh yez, so eh
couldnt liff um up no mo.

Dat de way Buh Rabbit tek eh rewenge on Buh Elephunt case eh mash eh chillun, an dat de reason huccum Buh Elephunt hab flop yez tel ter-day.

XXXVIII

BUH RABBIT, BUH WOLF, AN BUH POSSUM.

Buh Rabbit an Buh Wolf gone long de ribber bank fuh hunt Cooter agg. Dem Cooter blan come outer de water wen de tide high, an dig hole een de san, an lay dem agg, an kibber dem ober so crow an ting cant fine um. Buh Rabbit an Buh Wolf come topper nough er Cooter nes, an dem gedder de agg an share um equel. Dem pit um een bag, an es dem gin gwine home, de agg so fresh an sweet, Buh Rabbit slip eh han een eh bag an onbeknowinst ter Buh Wolf eh suck all de agg wuh bin fall ter him share befo dem retch de fork er de road way dem gwine part compny.

Buh Wolf tote all him agg home, an gen um ter him wife. Eh yent bin een eh house berry long wen up come Buh Rabbit duh puff an der blow. Soon es eh ketch eh bref eh say: "Buh Wolf, wuh you bin do long dem Cooter agg? Enty you fine out say dem spile? Me bin gib some er mine ter me wife, an eh gen um cramp colic right off. Me run all de way fuh tell you, so you kin sabe you fambly from sick."

Buh Wolf nebber spicion say Buh Rabbit bin er tell um lie, an eh tenk um berry much, an eh gone git de Cooter agg an trow um way. Buh Rabbit notus way Buh Wolf bin trow de agg; an soon es Buh Wolf gone back een him house, Buh Rabbit gedder dem up an tote um off een de bush, an seddown an biggin fuh eat dem dist es saterfy es kin be.

Eh so happne say Buh Wolf come pon topper Buh Rabbit duh eat dem Cooter agg, an eh see right off how Buh Rabbit done fool um. Eh git rale mad, an eh mek eh jump fuh graff Buh Rabbit, but Buh Rabbit too quick fur um, and eh tek ter eh heel. Buh Wolf push um so tight eh mek um quit de groun an tek ter one pussimmon tree. Buh Rabbit so light eh gone out on one leely limb way Buh Wolf couldnt foller um ner retch um. Wen Buh Wolf fine out eh couldnt pit eh han pon topper Buh Rabbit fuh lick um, eh call ter Buh Possum, wuh bin hab house close by, an eh ax um fuh run day an watch Buh Rabbit tel him coulder git him ax fuh cut down de tree an ketch Buh Rabbit. Buh Possum come, an eh seddown onder de tree duh gard Buh Rabbit wile Buh Wolf gone fuh him ax.

Arter er wile Buh Rabbit say: "Buh Possum, dem yer pussimmon berry sweet.

Enty you want some?" Buh Possum, him mek answer: "Yes, me Budder, me berry lub pussimmon, an me will glad fuh git some." Den Buh Rabbit tell um fuh step ter him house an fetch eh fanner fuh ketch de pussimmon es eh pick um an drap um. Buh Possum so anxious fuh tase de pussimmon eh clean furgit wuh Buh Wolf bin leff um fuh do, an so eh gone ter him house fuh git eh fanner. Soon es eh back tun, Buh Rabbit slip down de tree an lean fuh home. Wen Buh Wolf come wid eh ax, eh fine Buh Rabbit an Buh Possum all two gone. Eh dat bex eh dunno wuffer do. Een er leely wile yuh come Buh Possum duh tote he fanner. Buh Wolf questun um, an wen eh fine out how Buh Rabbit done fool um an git way, eh tun een an cuss Buh Possum an beat um. Eh tek a smart somebody fuh head Buh Rabbit.

XXXIX.

BUH RABBIT, BUH WOLF, AN DE HOLLER TREE.

Arter Buh Rabbit bin fool Buh Wolf bout dem Cooter agg, an slip way from Buh Possum, eh faid fuh meet Buh Wolf, an eh walk berry skittish ebry time eh lef eh house. Buh Wolf bin on de keen look-out fuh um. One day dem meet. Buh Wolf, him say: "Haw! Budder, me got you now. You dodge me long time. Ebry man fuh isself." Wid dat eh tek arter Buh Rabbit. Buh Rabbit, him bin quaintun wid all de holler tree een de wood, an wen Buh Wolf push um close, eh jump een one er dem. Buh Wolf run up an eh say: "Me got you now. Come out an tek you lick, er me gwine bun you up een dis tree." Eh no bin know say narrur holler bin on tarruh side er de tree, an dat Buh Rabbit done run clean tru an gone. Wen eh couldnt yeddy nuttne from Buh Rabbit, Buh Wolf gedder fat pine tick, an eh poke um een de holler an eh pit fire ter um. De fire roll, an Buh Wolf feed um tell de tree bun down. Eh saterfy say Buh Rabbit done bun up, an eh gone home, an eh mek brag ter him fambly say him bin stroy Buh Rabbit.

108

Eh yent bin tree day arter dat wen lo
an behole! Buh Wolf meet Buh Rabbit
duh seddown een de big road, dist es content
es ef nuttne bin happne, duh leek isself.
Buh Wolf hail um an eh say: "Buh Rabbit, dat duh you? Enty me bin bun you up
tarruh day? Why you duh do duh leek
youself so happy an content?" Buh Rabbit, him mek answer: "Budder, dat holler
way you bin try fuh bun me een, gone ter
de top er de tree, an eh bin full er honey.
De fire melt de honey, an eh run down an
kibber me all ober. Me yent done git um
all offer me tel now. You come tase me an
see how sweet me yiz." Buh Wolf so lub
honey eh furgit eh spite gainst Buh Rabbit,
an eh come up an eh taste um, an eh fine out
say honey bin all ober Buh Rabbit. Den eh
ax Buh Rabbit fuh show um one holler way
him kin git some honey. Buh Rabbit gree
fuh do so ef Buh Wolf would mek fren wid
um. Dem shake han, and den Buh Rabbit
tell Buh Wolf fuh foller um. Eh tek um ter
one tree wuh hab holler on one side, but wuh
shet up on tarruh side, an eh tell Buh Wolf
say dat tree full er honey, an eh mus git een
an crawl up nigh de top es eh could go.
Buh Wolf trus Buh Rabbit, an eh gone een

de holler. Soon es eh git een, Buh Rabbit tek one lightwood knot an eh chink up de hole so Buh Wolf couldnt come out. Den eh gedder some fat pine, an eh mek fire an eh bun Buh Wolf up een de holler. While eh duh bun, Buh Wolf bague an pray Buh Rabbit fuh leh um come out, but Buh Rabbit wouldnt yeddy um.

Buh Rabbit leetle fuh true an eh yent strong, but eh berry scheemy an eh hab er bad heart.

XL

BUH RABBIT AN DE CUNJUR MAN.

Buh Rabbit greedy fuh hab mo sense den all de tarruh animel. Eh yent lub fuh wuk, an eh try heap er scheme fuh git eh libbin outer edder people by fool um.

One time eh gone ter one wise Cunjur Man fuh larne um him way, an fuh git him knowledge, so him kin stonish tarruh people an mek dem bliebe say him bin wise mo ner ebrybody. De Cunjur Man larne um heap er curous ting. At las Buh Rabbit ax um fuh gen um eh full knowledge. De Cunjur Man say: "Buh Rabbit, you hab sense nough aready." Buh Rabbit keep on bague um, an den de Cunjur Man mek answer: "Ef you kin ketch one big rattlesnake an fetch um ter me live, me gwine do wuh you ax me fuh do."

Buh Rabbit git ehself one long stick an eh gone der wood. Eh hunt tel eh fine one whalin ob er rattlesnake duh quile up on one log. Eh pass de time er day berry perlite wid um, an arterwards eh bet de snake say him yent bin es long as de stick wuh him hab een him han. Buh Rattlesnake laugh at um, an eh mek answer dat eh know eh yiz long mo na de stick. Fuh settle de bet Buh Rattlesnake tretch ehself out ter eh berry lenk on de log, an Buh Rabbit pit de pole long side er um fuh medjuh um. Man sir! befo Buh Rattlesnake fine out, Buh Rabbit slip one noose roun eh neck an fastne um tight ter de een der de pole. Buh Rattlesnake twis ehself, an wrop ehself roun an roun de pole, an try fuh git eh head loose, but all eh twis an tun yent do um no good. An so Buh Rabbit ketch um, an cahr um ter de Cunjur Man.

De Cunjur Man rale suprise, an eh say: "Buh Rabbit, me always bin yeddy say you bin hab heap er sense, but now me know dat you got um. Ef you kin fool Rattlesnake, you hab all de sense you want." Wen Buh Rabbit keep on bague de Cunjur Man fuh gie um mo sense, de Cunjur Man answer: "You go fetch me er swarm er Yaller Jacket, an wen you bring um ter me, me prommus you teh gie you all de sense you want."

Ebrybody know say Yaller Jacket wus den warse, an bee, an hornet. Eh sting so bad, an eh berry lub fuh drap topper ebryting wuh come close eh nes, an dout gie um any warnin. So wuh Buh Rabbit do? Eh gone an eh git one big calabash, an eh crape um out clean, an eh cut one hole een um, an eh pit honey een um, an eh tie um on de een er one long pole. Den eh hunt tel eh fine er Yaller Jacket nes, an eh set de calabash close by um dout worry de Yaller Jacket, an eh leff um day, an eh tan off an watch um. Bimeby de Yaller Jacket scent de honey, an dem come out de nes an gone een de calabash fuh eat de honey. Wen de calabash full er Yaller Jacket, Buh Rabbit slip up an stop de hole, an cahr um ter de Cunjur Man. De Cunjur Man mek er great miration ober wuh Buh Rabbit bin done, an eh say: "Buh Rabbit, you is suttenly de smartest ob all de animel, an you sense shill git mo an mo ebry day. Mo na dat, me gwine pit white spot on you forrud, so ebrybody kin see you hab de bes sense een you head." An dat de way Buh Rabbit come fuh hab er leely tuff er white hair between eh yez.

XLI.

BUH RABBIT, BUH FOX, AN DE FISHERMAN.

Buh Rabbit es er soon man. You haffer git up befo day fuh head um. Wayebber you fine um, eh yez cock up fuh yeddy ebryting wuh duh gwine on. Eh nose duh twis from side ter side fuh ketch all de scent duh float een de element, an wen eh walk bout eh hop so light you tink der sperit. Eh lub fuh lib close big road an settlement, way him kin quaintun wid all wuh happne, an pick eh chance fuh mek eh libbin easy.

One time er Ole Man hab er fish trap wuh mek wid bode. Eh hab er gate. Wen de tide duh come een de creek, de gate open an leh de fish een; an wen de tide duh gwine back der ribber, de gate shet an stop all de fish wuh day een de creek. Ebry low tide de Ole Man tek eh leely waggin an wisit eh trap, an collec de fish an pit um een eh waggin an cahr um home fuh him an eh fambly fuh eat.

Buh Rabbit watch de Ole Man es eh pass day arter day long de big road, an eh hanker arter de fish, but eh yent know rightly how fuh git some. Arter er wile eh fix dis plan. De nex time eh see de Ole Man duh comin

114

long de road wid eh waggin an fish, eh leddown dist on de adge er de road, an eh pant
same luk eh bin gwine fuh dead. Es de ole
man bin er pass long eh notus um, an eh
stop, an eh gone ter um an eh ax um wuh ail
um. Buh Rabbit mek answer een er woice
so leely you cacely kin yeddy um, an tell um
say eh berry sick; dat eh bin gwine home
wen eh back an eh leg gie out, an eh couldnt
trabble no furder. Den eh bague de Ole
Man fuh tek um up een eh waggin an cahr
um long de big road tel eh come ter de place
way him fuh tun off fuh gwine ter him house.
De Ole Man gree fuh do so, an eh liff Buh
Rabbit up, an eh pit um een eh waggin long
side de pile er fish. Buh Rabbit leddown
luk eh dead. De Ole Man back tun ter Buh
Rabbit. Een er leely while Buh Rabbit
biggin fuh slip fish outer de waggin, an trow
um, onbeknowinst ter de Ole Man, een de
bush wuh bin er grow long side er de road.
Wen dem mose git ter de place way de Ole
Man gwine tun out de big road, Buh Rabbit hop outer de waggin dout de Ole Man
shum, an run back an gedder all de fish wuh
him bin tief.

Es de Ole Man retch eh big gate, eh look
behine fuh see how Buh Rabbit duh mek

out; an de fus ting eh know Buh Rabbit yent day een de waggin, an heap er him fish done missin. Den de Ole Man fine out say Buh Rabbit bin fool um an tief eh fish. De Ole Man berry bex, an eh dribe home an tell eh wife bout de ting.

Arter Buh Rabbit done gedder de fish wuh eh bin tief outer de Ole Man waggin, eh pit um on tring, an eh start fuh tote um ter him house. Buh Fox meet um, an eh quire way eh git all dem fish. Buh Rabbit up an tell um. Buh Fox say him want git some too. Den Buh Rabbit mek um senserble wen de Ole Man gwine come long de road, an eh show um good place fuh him fuh wuk eh plan fuh do dist es him bin do.

De nex day Buh Fox tek eh stan sider de big road an wait fuh de Ole Man an eh waggin. Befo long yuh eh come. Buh Fox trow isself in de groun, an roll ober, an moan berry pitiful. De Ole Man shum, an eh light offer eh waggin an run up ter um wid eh big whip een eh han. Buh Fox bin tink say de Ole Man gwine pity um, an tek um een eh waggin same luk eh done Buh Rabbit. Steader dat, an befo eh fine out, de Ole Man knock um een de head wid de butt er eh whip an stunted um. Den eh

beat um ter det, an eh tek um up an eh trow
um een eh waggin, an eh dribe home. Wen
eh git day eh call eh wife an eh show um de
tief wuh bin tek eh fish. De Ole Man yent
bin know de diffunce tween Buh Rabbit an
Buh Fox. Eh tink all two bin de same animel.

Buh Rabbit, him no care so eh sabe isself.
Him bin know say Buh Fox gwine ketch
de debble wen de Ole Man come pon topper
um.

XLII.

Buh Rabbit an Buh Wolf come inter cohoot fuh kill cow. Dem gone een de paster
an pick out one fat yearlin, an run um down,
an ketch um, an cut eh troat. Den dem
skin um an share de meat. Buh Wolf claim
de bigges part, case him hab de bigges fambly. Eh strong mo ner Buh Rabbit, an so
Buh Rabbit yent hab de power fuh mek um
do jestice. But ef Buh Wolf hab de strenk,
Buh Rabbit hab de bes sense. So wuh Buh
Rabbit do? Eh tek some salt outer him bag,
an eh buil fire, an eh brile some er de yearlin meat on de coals, an eh eat um right befo
Buh Wolf. Soon es eh done eat um, eh cry
out an eh say eh hab pain er belly, an eh
double ehself all up, an eh roll eh yeye, an
eh waller all long de groun, an eh mek all
sorter curous motion an noise. Buh Wolf
skaid, an eh conclude say de meat yent good.
Eh tink say eh pizen Buh Rabbit, an dem
gree fuh leff um.

Buh Wolf wait tel Buh Rabbit sorter
come teh, an den eh help um ter him house
an tell um goodbye.

Wen sun down an eh biggin fuh dark,
Buh Rabbit gedder him fambly, and dem

gone an git de yearlin meat, an dem cahr um home an dem eat um. Nuttne bin ail de meat. Eh bin soun an sweet, an Buh Rabbit do dis fuh fool Buh Wolf an git him share too.

XLIII.

Arter dat time wen Buh Rabbit bin play dat trick on Buh Wolf an ride um up ter de Gal house wuh dem all two bin er cote, Buh Wolf berry bex long Buh Rabbit, an eh wan ketch um fuh gie um good lickin. Buh Rabbit, him so smate eh keep outer Buh Wolf way so eh couldnt come pon topper um. Buh Wolf hire one dog fuh help um ketch Buh Rabbit. One day de Dog meet Buh Rabbit der wood, an dout say one wud ter um, eh lean arter um fuh ketch um. Buh Rabbit run, but de Dog push um so tight Buh Rabbit, fuh sabe ehself, jump een one holler oak tree. De hole bin too leely fuh de Dog fuh foller um, an so Buh Rabbit mek ehself saterfy say eh done git way. Bimeby eh yeddy de Dog call one goose, an tell um fuh watch de holler tel him kin git some fire an moss fuh smoke Buh Rabbit outer de tree. Wen de Dog gone fuh gedder de moss an git de fire, Buh Rabbit call ter de Goose an ax um: "How you duh watch me wen you no see me?" Wid dat de Goose poke eh long head een de holler fuh look fuh Buh Rabbit. Es eh do dat, Buh Rabbit trow rotten wood een eh yeye. Eh bline de Goose, an eh draw eh head out, an wile eh duh fight fuh git de rotten wood outer eh yeye Buh Rabbit slip out an gone. Wen de Dog come back, eh stuff de moss een de holler, an eh pit fire ter um, an eh mek er hebby smoke; but eh cant see ner yeddy nuttne bout Buh Rabbit. Den eh biggin fuh spicion say Buh Rabbit might er git out, an eh tackle de Goose bout um. Eh notus de Goose yeye red an eh duh run water. De Goose tell um how Buh Rabbit bin trow rotten wood een eh yeye wen eh bin er peep up de holler. Den de Dog know fuh sutten say Buh Rabbit bin wuk dat plan fuh git way, an dat eh done gone fuh true. Eh so bex eh cuss de Goose fuh er fool, an eh tun on um fuh stroy um. De Goose holler, an manage fuh sail way een de element, but eh leff eh fedder een de Dog mouf.

XLIV.

BUH SQUIRLE AN BUH FOX.

Buh Squirle bin berry busy duh gedder hickry not on de groun fuh pit way fuh feed ehself an eh fambly duh winter time. Buh Fox bin er watch um, an befo Buh Squirle shum, eh slip up an eh graff um. Buh Squirle, eh dat skaid eh trimble all ober, an eh bague Buh Fox fuh lem go. Buh Fox tell um say eh bin er try fuh ketch um long time, but eh hab sich sharp yeye, an keen yez, an spry leg, eh manage fuh dodge um; an now wen eh got um at las, eh mean fuh kill um an eat um. Wen Buh Squirle fine out dat Buh Fox yent bin gwine pity um an tun um loose, but dat eh fix fuh kill um an eat um, Buh Squirle say teh Buh Fox: "Enty you know say nobody oughter eat eh bittle befo eh say grace ober um?" Buh Fox him mek answer: "Dat so;" an wid dat eh pit Buh Squirle een front er um, an eh fall on eh knee, an eh kibber eh yeye wid eh han, an eh tun een fuh say grace.

Wile Buh Fox bin er do dis, Buh Squirle manage fuh slip way; an wen Buh Fox open eh yeye, eh see Buh Squirle duh run up de tree way him couldnt tetch um.

Buh Fox fine eh couldnt help ehself, an eh call arter Buh Squirle an eh say: "Nummine, Boy, you done git way now, but de nex time me clap dis han topper you, me gwine eat you fus an say grace arterward."

Bes plan fuh er man fuh mek sho er eh bittle befo eh say tenky fuh um.

XLV.

BUH RABBIT, BUH WOLF, AN DE BUCKRA MAN.

Er Buckra man bin hab er gang er sheep.
Ebry now an den eh miss one. Eh sarche
eh fiel, an eh see Buh Wolf track day, an
eh mek up eh mine say him bin er de one
wuh duh tief eh sheep. Eh fix heaper plan
fuh ketch um, but eh fail. At lenk eh call
een Buh Rabbit, case eh hab summuch
sense, fuh help um. Buh Rabbit, him gree
fuh do so ef de Buckra man would len um
one horse, an would prommus no fuh tell
Buh Wolf nuttne bout de ting.

De Buckra man gen um de prommus an
len um de horse. Buh Rabbit ride de horse
ter him house, an eh sen wud ter Buh Wolf
say him dist bin buy er fine ridin horse, an
him want um fuh come an tek er ride long
um. Buh Wolf, him come, an wen eh look
topper de horse eh tell Buh Rabbit him
would lub fuh ride um, but dat him faid say
de horse gwine fling um. Buh Rabbit mek
answer say him mussnt faid; dat him gwine
pit saddle on de horse, an wen Buh Wolf
git een um eh gwine tie eh leg so him cant
fall off; an, mo ner dat, him gwine git up

behine fuh hole um on. Arter dat Buh
Wolf seem saterfy.

Buh Rabbit trow de saddle on de horse an
gelt um tight. Den Buh Wolf climb up an
tek eh seat. Buh Rabbit tek string, an eh
tie Buh Wolf leg fas ter de stirrup. Now
eh say: "Me gwine git up behine fuh hole
you on." Steader dat, wen Buh Wolf yent
bin er notus, eh step back, an eh tek er
bunch er cock-spur an eh lick um onder de
horse tail. De ting hot de animel so bad, eh
jump, an eh pitch, an eh kick up. Buh
Wolf grab de bridle an juk de horse mouf,
an dat mek um rare up. Buh Wolf git rale
skaid, an eh holler fuh Buh Rabbit fuh tek
um off. Buh Rabbit tell um fuh hole on
tel him kin onloose de saddle. All dis time
de horse bin er cut sich caper Buh Wolf
couldnt manage um, an so eh drap de bridle
an heng on ter eh mange fuh keep from fall
off. Wen de horse fine say eh head loose,
eh mek fuh home; an befo Buh Wolf fine
out eh run tru de big gate an roun de
house ter de stable. De Buckra man bin er
set een eh piazza, an eh see wen de horse
come up wid Buh Wolf der heng topper eh
neck. Eh run ter de stable, an eh leh de
horse an Buh Wolf een. Den eh call eh

driber, an dem ontie Buh Wolf an fastne um ter one tree. Arter dem bin gen um bout one hundud lash, Buh Rabbit run up an bague de Buckra man fuh tun Buh Wolf loose. Eh did tun um loose. Buh Wolf nebber did fine out say Buh Rabbit bin fix dis plan fuh pit um een de Buckra man han, an eh tell Buh Rabbit heap er tenky fuh de faber wuh him bin done ter um.

Ebry time you yeddy bout Buh Rabbit you fine um duh come out head.

XLVI.

Buh Rabbit fool Buh Wolf so many time, an een sich diffrunt fashion, dat eh outdone wid um. Ebry time eh try fuh ketch um fuh lick um, Buh Rabbit somehow er narruh slip tru eh han an git way. Buh Wolf, him hire edder people fuh wuk plan fuh git de better er Buh Rabbit an pit um een eh power, but, bless you soul! dem fail too, an Buh Rabbit, him go clear. De ting mose worry Buh Wolf life outer um. Eh fret so bout um tel eh biggin fuh tun rale po.

At lenk Buh Wolf gie out say him berry sick. Leely wile arter dat, de news come dat Buh Wolf dead. Eh wife eenwite all eh fren ter de funeral. Buh Wolf mek sho say eh gwine ketch Buh Rabbit now.

Buh Bear, him bin der de passon. Dog come. Roccoon come. Squirle come. Possum come. Cow come. Alligatur an Cooter, dem come. Deer, him bin day too. Buh Wolf, him bin er lay out on er bench een de middle er him house, kibber ober wid er wite clorte, an eh wife an eh chillun duh tan roun um duh cry. Buh Owl, him fetch

127

er spade fuh dig de grabe, an bud bin day too fuh sing er hyme.

Wen dem all bin gedder, Buh Rabbit enter dist es careful, an tek eh stan jes by de do. Dem wait leely wile fuh Buh Fox, but him sen wud say him wife hab feber an him couldnt leff um. Den Buh Bear, him tek eh book an eh read um, an eh preach er sarmint. Arter dat de Mockinbud raise er chune, an dem all sing.

All dis time Buh Wolf bin er leddown, tretch out ter eh full lenk, and stiff lucker eh bin dead fuh true. Eh hole eh bref so tight, nobody could yeddy um breave. Wen de preachin an de singin done ober, dem all gone up fuh tek dem las look at Buh Wolf befo dem tote um out fuh bury um. Dem raise up de clorte wuh bin ober eh face, an eh look dist es natrul; an dem tell um goodbye one by one. Buh Rabbit him walk up las, an eh yent gone berry close needer. Buh Rabbit always tote eh good sense bout um, an eh nebber will run no resk. Es eh come fuh look topper Buh Wolf, Buh Wolf bin spec say eh woulder tan so close dat eh coulder graff um. But wen eh fine Buh Rabbit sorter skittish, an eh duh ease ehself off, eh tek de chance, an, all ob er

sutten, eh trow ehself offer de bench an eh
mek arter Buh Rabbit. Buh Rabbit, him
bin hab eh yeye on Buh Wolf all de time,
an befo Buh Wolf could mek eh way tru
de crowd an come up long um, Buh Rabbit
slip out de back do an trow ehself een de
brier patch, way Buh Wolf couldnt foller
um. De people all stonish, an wen dem fine
out de trute er de ting, dem berry bex; an,
befo dem leff, dem bemean Buh Wolf sich
er fashion eh bin shame fuh show ehself een
de settlement fuh many er days. Dat bin
er dutty trick wuh Buh Wolf play on eh
fren and on Buh Rabbit, but Buh Rabbit,
him outdo um.

XLVII.

Er New Nigger notus say eh Mossa heap er time duh seddown wid eh foot cross, yent duh say nuttne an yent duh do nuttne, wen him haffer wuk all de time. One day eh ax eh Mossa huccum dat. De Buckra man answer: "Wen you see me duh seddown, an you tink me duh lazy, same time me duh wuk long me head, an duh mek plan, an study pon ting."

Soon arter dat de Buckra man come pon topper de New Nigger een de fiel. De sun hot. Eh bin drap eh hoe, an bin er seddown on de cotton bed duh res ehself. De Buckra man git bex case de Nigger bin er glec eh wuk, an eh say ter um: "Huccum you stop de wuk wuh me bin gen you fuh do? Wuh mek you duh lazy disher fashion?" Den de New Nigger, him mek answer: "Mossa, me duh wuk long me head." Wen de Buckra man quire wuh kind er head wuk him duh do, de New Nigger say: "Mossa, ef you see tree pigeon duh set on dat tree limb, an you shoot an kill one er dem, how many gwine leff?" Eh Mossa reply: "Any fool kin tell dat. Ob scource

130

two gwine leff." De New Nigger, him mek answer: "No, Mossa, you miss. Ef you shoot an kill one er dem pigeon, de edder two boun fuh fly way, an none gwine leff."

De Buckra man bleege fuh laugh, an eh yent do nuttne ter de New Nigger case eh glec eh wuk.

XLVIII

BUH RABBIT AN DE KING DARTER.

Dere was er King wuh bin hab er pooty
Darter, an heap er people bin er cote um.
De gal couldnt mek up eh mine which one
fuh tek, an so eh ax eh farruh fuh help um
pick. Den eh farruh, wuh bin de King,
gen out wud say de one wuh kin fetch ter
um de Alligatur yeye teet, an water from de
Deer yeye, shill hab eh Darter.

All dem wuh bin er cote de gal fix plan
fuh git dem ting, but dem fail. Ebry body
bin faid Alligatur, an nobody could outrun
Buh Deer. Buh Rabbit, him bin berry lub
de gal, an him hanker arter marry um, so eh
study bout de ting an mek eh scheme. Eh
tek eh fiddle an eh gone ter de ribber bank,
an eh play er funny chune, an eh sing er
funny song. Buh Alligatur yeddy um; an
bimeby eh crawl outer de mash grass, an eh
leddown close by Buh Rabbit, so him kin
ketch all wuh Buh Rabbit der play an der
sing. Buh Rabbit do eh bes, an de ting
tickle Buh Alligatur so bad eh laugh berry
harty. Buh Rabbit play an sing, an pick eh
chance, an wen Buh Alligatur duh shet eh
yeye an open eh mout fuh laugh, eh tek eh

fiddle bow an, all ob er sutten, eh knock one
er Buh Alligatur yeye teet outer eh head.
Befo eh fine out, Buh Rabbit done pick up
de teet an gone.

Den Buh Rabbit notus way Buh Deer
blan ramble der wood, an eh dig er deep
hole, an eh kibber um ober complete long
dut, an pine straw, an oak leaf.   Eh hide
een de bush oneside duh watch.   Bimeby
Buh Deer, him come long duh eat grass, an
befo eh fine out, de groun gie way onder eh
foot, an eh drap bottom er de hole.   Buh
Deer dat skaid eh dunno wuffer do.   Eh
scuffle.   Eh holler, but eh couldnt git out.
Buh Rabbit run day, an eh tell um say dog
bin on eh track, an dat dem mose git day.
Wid dat Buh Deer gib up, an biggin fuh
cry.   Den Buh Rabbit, him slip een de hole
wid er leely calabash, an eh ketch de water
duh run down from Buh Deer yeye.   Arter
dat eh gone home, an eh tek de Alligatur
yeye teet, an de calabash wuh hab de Deer
yeye water een um, an eh light out fuh de
King house.

Wen him show de King wuh him bring,
de King gree say Buh Rabbit head er all
dem wuh bin er cote him Darter, an eh gen
um de gal, an dem bin hab er hebby weddin.

XLIX.

DE SINGLE BALL.

Er Buckra man bin berry lub fuh hunt
deer. Eh nussen fuh brag too. Eh hab er
Serbant wuh always gone wid um der wood
fuh dribe de deer. Him bin berry fond er
eh Mossa, an eh ready any time fuh schway
ter de tale wuh him tell bout how much deer
dem kill, an way dem shoot um. One time
dis Buckra man bin tell eh fren say him
shoot er deer long er rifle, an wen eh gone
fuh zamine um, eh fine say de ball shoot off
eh hine foot an hit um een eh yez. Him
fren couldnt see how dat happne, an dem
yent bin want fuh bleeve de tale. Den de
hunter man call pon topper him Serbant
fuh proobe wuh him bin say. De Serbant
speak de wud same luk him Mossa bin talk
um. Den de gentlemans ax um how de same
ball could er hit de deer een eh hine foot
an een eh yez same time. De Nigger
cratch eh head, an den eh mek answer:
"Gentlemans, me spec wen Mossa fire pon
topper um, de deer mus be bin er bresh fly
offer eh yez wid eh hine foot." Dat sorter
saterfy de gentlemans, an sabe de Buckra
man wud.

Arter de gentlemans done gone, de Serbant call eh Mossa one side an eh say: "Mossa, me willin fuh back anyting you say bout hunt an kill deer, but lemme bague you nex time you tell bout how you shoot um, you pit de hole closer. Dis time you mek um so fur apart, me hab big trouble fur git um togerruh."

L.

Buh Roccoon ax Buh Possum wuh mek, wen de dog tackle um, eh double up ehself, an kibber eh yeye wid eh han, an wunt fight lucker man an lick de dog off. Buh Possum grin eh teet same lucker fool, an eh say, wen de dog come pon topper um, dem tickle him rib so bad long dem mout dat him bleege ter laugh; an so him furgit fuh fight.

Coward man hab all kind er lie fuh tell fuh scuse ehself.

LI.

Buh Wolf bin er set een de do er him house duh play eh fiddle. Lord er massy! how dat animel did mek dat fiddle talk! Buh Wolf yeye shet tight, an eh dis bin er rock from side ter side, an draw eh bow teh eh berry lenk, en der pat de time wid eh foot. Er hebby shower er rain come on. Buh Rabbit, him bin een de big road not fur from Buh Wolf house. Buh Rabbit yent lub rain, an eh try fuh shelter ehself onder er oak tree wuh kibber wid long moss. De rain lick um een eh yez, an eh leff fuh hunt better place. Es eh pass by Buh Wolf house, eh notus Buh Wolf duh set een de do duh play eh fiddle. Buh Wolf so tek up wid eh play dat eh shet eh yeye an yent duh watch wuh gwine on roun um. So Buh Rabbit mek up eh mine fuh slip een de do pass Buh Wolf, an set een him house tel de rain done ober. Buh Rabbit foot so sofe nobody kin yeddy um wen eh walk. Him no know, but Buh Wolf ketch sight er um outer de corner ob him yeye wen Buh Rabbit hop een de do an run back side er de room. Eh sed down day an mek ehself saterfy, an duh wait top-

137

per de rain. Buh Wolf him yent leh Buh
Rabbit know say him shum, but eh biggin
fuh tun eh chune, an eh play an eh sing:
"Tenk God, rain done sen meat een me
house. Tenk God, rain done sen meat een
me house." Buh Rabbit yeddy; an eh spicion say Buh Wolf smell um, an fine out say
him bin een eh house. Buh Rabbit hair rise,
an eh want fuh git out, but eh faid fuh slip
back trough de do way Buh Wolf bin er sed
down. Buh Rabbit berry oneasy een eh
mine, an eh duh consider plan fuh mek eh
scape.

Buh Wolf house buil on de groun senker
hog pen. Eh mek wid pole. Him bin tink
say him got Buh Rabbit safe, an so eh keep
on play eh fiddle an sing: "Tenk God, rain
done sen meat een me house. Tenk God, rain
done sen meat een me house." Wile Buh
Wolf duh mek ehself saterfy say him hab
Buh Rabbit an gwine eat um soon es de rain
done ober, Buh Rabbit duh grabble, grabble, grabble onder de bottom er de pole, tel
eh mek hole big nough, an den eh slip out,
onbeknowinst teh Buh Wolf, an hop roun
teh de front do, an eh holler teh Buh Wolf:
"You duh sing an der play, 'Tenk God,
rain done sen meat een you house,' but you

yent eat um yet, an you yent gwine eat um."
Wid dat eh leff right befo Buh Wolf face.
Buh Wolf rale disappint.   Eh loss eh dinner.   Eh gone an eh heng up eh fiddle, an
eh say teh ehself: "Me tought sho me bin
hab um, but Rabbit beat my time."

LII

BUH ALLIGATUH, BUH RABBIT, AN BUH WOLF.

Buh Rabbit, him bin er tief Buh Alligatuh agg. Buh Alligatuh ketch um topper eh nes. Eh graff um an eh pit um een one crocus bag, an eh tie up de een er de bag tight, an eh heng um on one tree lim, an eh gone home fuh git eh lash fuh lick Buh Rabbit. Buh Rabbit dat skaid eh yeye big moner saucer. Eh duh trimble een de bag, an duh peep trough de crack een de crocus fuh notus wuh gwine happne.

Bimeby eh see Buh Wolf duh ramble dat way. Soon es Buh Wolf come anigh um, Buh Rabbit biggin fuh sing say him gwine teh Hebben, way him will hab nuttne fuh do cept joy ehself; way him will hab no corn fuh grine, no tetter fuh dig, no cotton fuh pick, no rice fuh hoe, an no chillun fuh mine. Buh Rabbit mek tense luk him so happy case de Lord dist er commin fuh tek um right up eenter de element.

Buh Wolf stop. Eh listne teh Buh Rabbit. Eh yeddy close, an den eh say: "Buh Rabbit, enty dat duh you woice?" Buh Rabbit, him mek answer: "Yes, Budder, dis duh me." Den Buh Wolf ax um wuh eh

duh do een dat crocus bag. Buh Rabbit tell
um say him dist fix ehself dat er way so de
Lord kin fine um handy fuh tek um right up
eenter Hebben; an den eh say: "Good-bye,
Buh Wolf, I leff all me trial behine; you
no gwine see me no mo; me gwine leff right
off fuh Hebben." Buh Wolf now, him yent
hab no better sense den fuh bleebe wuh Buh
Rabbit duh talk; an eh bague Buh Rabbit
fuh leh him jine um an go long um. Buh
Rabbit, him mek answer: "Me Budder, me
glad fuh bleege you, but de good Lord tell
me say only one at er time kin enter Hebben. Two an two cant go day." Buh Wolf
bague. Eh bague. At lenk Buh Rabbit
mek tense say eh gie way caze Buh Wolf
bague um so bad, an eh say: "Well, Budder, you seem so anxious me gwine leh you
tek me chance dis time, an me will haffer
wait topper de Lord tel narruh tun."

Wid dat eh tell Buh Wolf fuh loose de
bag offer de tree lim, an ontie um. Arter
Buh Wolf done do dis, Buh Rabbit git out,
an Buh Wolf tek eh place een de bag. Buh
Rabbit tie up de mout er de bag berry tight,
an heng um gen on de tree lim. Buh Wolf,
lucker fool, duh set eenside duh spec fuh
rise ter Hebben. Buh Rabbit now, eh so

glad eh free, eh hop off one side an hide ehself een one gall-berry ticket, way nobody
kin shum, an cock eh yez fuh notus wuh
gwine happne. Eh know say big trouble
gwine come topper Buh Wolf.

Eh yent bin berry long wen yuh come
Buh Alligatuh duh tote er keen black lash.
Eh gone right up ter de bag, an eh gen um
er nasty cut. Den eh haul back an eh gen
de bag anurrer whaling ub er lick. Eh no
bin know say Buh Rabbit bin git out, an dat
Buh Wolf bin eenside. Buh Wolf couldnt
mek out wuh bin gwine on. De lick hot um
so bad eh holler out: "Wudder dat? Who
duh dat? Wuh hoona duh do long me?
Lemme lone." Buh Alligatuh so bex eh
yent yeddy say eh bin Buh Wolf woice, an
eh keep duh pile on de lick tell eh tare de
crocus an cut de bag down. Buh Wolf all
lick up so eh casely kin walk. Wen eh
scuffle outer de bag, Buh Alligatuh fine out
fuh de fus time say eh binner whale up Buh
Wolf, steader Buh Rabbit wuh bin tief eh
agg. Den Buh Alligatuh ax Buh Wolf par-
don, an mek um tell um huccum Buh Rabbit
bin fool um an git um fuh tek eh place een
de bag. Buh Alligatuh bex an sorry all
two: eh bex caze Buh Rabbit play dat trick

an git way; eh sorry caze Buh Wolf beat up so sewere. All dis time Buh Rabbit duh squat een de bush, way eh kin see an yeddy ebry ting, duh half kill ehself wid laugh.

All de sorry wuh Buh Alligatuh bin sorry fuh Buh Wolf yent bin done um no good. Eh bin bruise up so bad eh haffer tek eh bed fuh mona two week, an all dat time Buh Wolf fambly mose dead long hongry.

Buh Alligatuh an Buh Wolf all two mek plan fuh ketch Buh Rabbit, but dem nebber did obertek um. No matter wuh de trouble, Buh Rabbit always hab sense nough fuh clear ehself. Eh yent hab dem long yez an big yeye fuh nuttne.

LIII.

DE DYIN BULL-FROG.

One time er ole Bull-Frog bin berry sick an spectin fuh dead. All eh fren een de pon collec roun um an eh fambly, fuh nuss um an tek dem las look at um. Dat ole Frog bin hab er noung wife an heap er leely chillun. Eh berry trouble een eh breas bout who gwine mine eh fambly arter eh gone. Wen eh woice biggin fuh fail um, an dist befo eh dead, eh say: "Me fren, who gwine tek me wife wen de breaf leff dis yer body?" Eh fren all holler out at de top er dem woice: "Me me. Me me. Me me." Den eh quire: "Who er you gwine mine me leely chillun?" Fuh some time eh yent yeddy no answer; an den de answer come back ter um one by one from all ober de pon, an een er deep woice: "Yent der me. Yent der me. Yent der me."

Heap er people willin fuh notus er pooty noung widder, wen dem no want bodder long narruh man chillun.

LIV

BUH RABBIT, BUH PATTRIDGE, AN DE COW.

Buh Rabbit, him berry greedy, an him lub fuh tell lie. Him an Buh Pattridge mek greement fuh kill Cow. Buh Pattridge ax Buh Rabbit: "Way we gwine butcher um?" Buh Rabbit say: "Less we dribe um close up ter my house befo we kill um." Dem done dat, an arter dem kill an skin de Cow, dem cut um up fuh share um. Den Buh Rabbit tell Buh Pattridge: "You tek one er de fore-quarter, caze you know you leetle an cant tote much one time, an me radder you tek de fore-quarter anyhow, caze eh nex de heart, an eh mo sweeter den de res er de meat." So Buh Pattridge tek one er de fore-quarter an leff fuh him house.

Soon es Buh Pattridge gone duh tote eh meat home, Buh Rabbit tun een an tote all de res er de Cow ter him house, an pit um een eh room, an lock de do. Den eh stan outside duh watch fuh see wen Buh Pattridge would er come back fuh mo meat, so dem all two could er meet same time at de place way dem bin butcher de Cow. Buh Rabbit leh Buh Pattridge git er leely way ahead er um es dem gwine back ter de spot way de Cow bin kill, an wen eh come up eh say: "Hi! Buh Pattridge, way all de meat gone?" Buh Pattridge, him mek answer: "Me dis bin gwine ax you wuh you bin do wid all de meat." Buh Rabbit say: "How you kin ax me sich er question, wen me bin see er whole gang er Pattridge dis gone from yuh? Me sho say you an you fambly bin come back fuh tek anarruh tun long de meat." Buh Pattridge mek answer say him an eh fambly nebber bin nigh de Cow sence eh fus leff um. Den Buh Rabbit schway say: "Ef eh yender you, somebody else muster tief de Cow meat wen we all two bin gone;" an so eh fool Buh Pattridge, an mek um bleebe say strange people muster slip up an cahr off de meat, wen all de time him binner de tief, an hab um lock up safe een him house.

You nebber kin trus Buh Rabbit. Eh all fuh ehself; an ef you listne ter him tale, eh gwine cheat you ebry time, an tell de bigges lie dout wink eh yeye.

LV.

Long time ago dere bin er Ebo man wuh
bin er great fiddler. Eh know better den
all dem tarruh people wuffer do long fiddle.
Wen eh lean back, an shet eh yeye, an draw
eh bow fuh tru, nobody wuh yeddy kin
keep from shuffle eh foot. Ebry body roun
de settlement blan gage um fuh mek de
music fuh dem fuh dance. One day eh bin
gwine fuh keep eh gagement fuh play at er
party. Eh hab eh fiddle een er bag. Es
eh bin der walk tru er deep swamp, Buh
Tiger an Buh Bear tek eh track an run um.
De man skaid wus den bad, but eh wunt
drap eh fiddle. Eh clime one tree an fix ehself een one crotch. Fus ting eh know, Buh
Tiger biggin fuh crawl up de tree fuh ketch
um. De man holler and try fuh skaid de
beas, but eh wunt skaid. Eh keep on duh
clime up. Den de man draw eh fiddle an
eh bow outer de bag, an biggin fuh play wid
all eh strenk. Buh Tiger bleege fuh stop
teh listne ter um. Een er leely wile de chune
sweeten Buh Tiger so bad eh forgit ter foller
de man, an eh tun roun an come down de
tree, an him an Buh Bear graff han, an all

147

two set een fuh dance. De faster de fiddler
play, de faster dem dance. Dem gone roun
an roun, up an down, tel dem dead tired.
At lenk dem all two so outdone dem bleege
fuh drap der groun an try fuh ketch dem win.
Dem cant dance er foot furder, an dem duh
try fuh keep de time long dem head.

Wen de Fiddler notus how complete dem
outdone, eh slip down de tree, an tek eh foot
een eh han, an lean fuh de place way eh bin
gwine. Buh Tiger an Buh Bear yent hab
strenk fuh foller um: an so eh music sabe
um.

LVI

DE OLE KING AN DE NOUNG KING.

Er ole King yeddy say dem gwine pit er noung King een him place. De ting worry um an mek um bex. Eh want fuh keep eh trone: so eh gen order teh eh head man fuh mek him soldier kill all de ole people een de nation, so de noung King shant hab no wise pusson fuh help um cahr on de bidness er de kingdom. De soldier tek dem gun an dem club, an dem massacree all de ageable people een de lan.

Den de ole King sen wud teh de noung King, wuh de people bin pick out fuh rule ober dem, dat eh mus fetch um er fat hog, but eh musnt be eider er sow-hog, neider er bo-hog, but eh mus be er fat hog.

Wen de noung King git de message, eh tun dis answer: "Tell de ole King say me hab er fat barruh een de pen, an him mus come fur um; but eh musnt come een de day, ner eh musnt come fuh um een de night." De ole King, wen eh yeddy dis message, mek up eh mine say de noung King mus hab heap er sense, er else some wise man muster help um; an eh couldnt see how dat kin be, case all de ole an de wise people een de nation done kill. Eh no bin know dat wen de order gie fuh stroy all de ole people een de kingdom, de noung King hide eh farruh een one holler tree, an so eh mek eh scape from de soldier, an bin day fuh gen eh son sense.

De noung King tun sich er smart answer, wid de help er eh farruh, dat de ole King couldnt mek out wuh time fuh gone fuh de fat hog; an so eh gib up, an de noung King, befo long, come an tun um out an tek eh office.

LVII.

BUH GOAT AN BUH WOLF.

Buh Goat berry faid tunder an lightnin
an rain. One day big tunder storm rise een
de wes, an eh rain, an eh lightnin, an eh
hail. Buh Goat an eh wife bin er feed een
de wood close by Buh Wolf house. Wen
de lightnin flash, an de tunder roll, an de
rain po down, dem faid fuh stay een de
wood, an dem run teh Buh Wolf house, an
dem bague um fuh leh dem come een tel de
storm done ober. Buh Wolf tell dem yes;
an eh tun Buh Goat an eh wife een de shedroom, an eh shet de do behine dem an latch
um. Buh Wolf shedroom yent bin hab bode
flo. Eh mek topper de neked dut. Arter
Buh Wolf done shet up Buh Goat an eh wife,
eh git eh fiddle an eh biggin fuh play an
sing: "Tenky goolly God, tunder an lightnin done sen meat een me house. Tenky
goolly God, tunder an lightnin done sen meat
een me house." Buh Goat wife yeddy wuh
Buh Wolf bin er play an sing, an eh say
teh eh husbun: "Enty you yeddy wuh Buh
Wolf duh play an duh sing: 'Tenky goolly
God, tunder an lightnin done sen meat een
me house'? Him gwine kill an eat we. Bet-

ter leh we grabble out an leff." All dis time
Buh Wolf wife bin er tell eh husbun: "You
better mine wuh you duh sing. You better
keep you mout shet. Buh Goat an eh wife
gwine yeddy wuh you duh say." Buh Wolf
wouldnt listen ter um. Eh wouldnt stop.
Him say de rain duh fall so hebby Buh Goat
an him wife couldnt mek out wuh him duh
sing. Wile dis bin er gwine on, Buh Goat
an eh wife busy duh grabble, grabble, grabble onder de sill er de shedroom tel dem mek
hole big nough fuh dem fuh crawl out, an
den dem slip out an gone.

Wen de rain stop, Buh Wolf heng up eh
fiddle an gone git eh knife, an pit eh pot on
de fire, en sharpen eh knife on de pot rim.
Den eh onlatch de shedroom do an gone een
fuh cut de troat er Buh Goat an eh wife. De
fus ting eh fine out, Buh Goat an eh wife done
gone. Eh holler back ter him wife an eh
say: "Ole ooman! Buh Goat an eh wife git
way." De ole ooman—wuh bin Buh Wolf
wife—mek answer: "Enty me bin tell you
say Buh Goat an eh wife gwine yeddy? Duh
you mek dat. Ef you bin do es me bin tell
you, an keep you big mout shet, you bin hab
um all two now." Den Buh Wolf an eh
wife biggin fuh quarrel an fight caze Buh

152

Wolf skaid Buh Goat an eh wife an lem git way. Buh Wolf wife lick eh husbun tel eh holler, an eh tell um eh shant stay een de house bedout eh fine um een meat. Buh Wolf bague berry hard, an eh prommus say ef eh wife lem go him will hunt an fetch bittle right off. Den eh wife tun um loose, an Buh Wolf gone fuh git meat.

Een de arternoon er de same day, wile Buh Wolf bin er hunt bittle, eh meet up wid Buh Goat, an eh ax um: "Buh Goat, wuh sort er mean trick dat wuh you bin do me dis mornin?" Buh Goat, him bex, an him mek answer: "How you hab de face fuh talk long me an ax me sich er question? Enty you bin fix fuh kill me an me wife dis mornin arter you done gie we de freedom er you house? Enty we yeddy you sing an tenk de Lord case tunder an lightnin sen meat een you house? You hab er bad heart. You no duh frien." Buh Wolf, him say: "You mek mistake. Me no bin gwine hot you. Me dist bin er fun." Buh Goat answer: "Yes, you yiz bin mek up you mine fuh kill we. Haw Buck! me lub my life dist es much es you lub yourn, an me no want hab nuttne mo fuh do long you." Wen Buh Wolf fine eh couldnt fool Buh Goat, eh change eh chune an eh say: "Go long, Boy. You git way one time, but narruh chance gwine come; an de nex time me git you een me power me yent gwine wait topper nuttne, but me gwine pick you bone right off." Buh Goat laugh at um, an eh answer: "Now you done speak you mine, lemme tell you, you nebber gwine git narruh chance fuh ketch me. Me boun fuh watch you." An so dem part company. Buh Goat nebber did trus Buh Wolf from dat day tel dis.

LVIII.

The incident which we relate occurred some forty years ago at one of those beautiful plantations in the swamp-region of Georgia, where the magnolia grandiflora and the live-oak mingled their noble shadows,— where the cultivation of rice and sea-island cotton engaged the attention of the agriculturalist,—where generous hospitality and a patriarchal civilization abode,—and where, at a remove from city, all operations were conducted within the limits of the liberal domain, and through the intervention of means and servants appurtenant to the long-established and abundant home.

Prominent among the domestics on this plantation was Daddy Jack. A favorite servant, intelligent, obedient, courteous, and with the manners of the old school, he was now verging upon sixty. Among other duties devolved upon him was the general supervision of the plantation infirmary where the sick were carefully nursed and supplied with medicine and suitable food. Acquiring considerable knowledge in the treatment of ordinary diseases incident to climate and

155

exposure, he had become, in the estimation of his fellow-servants, a famous leech; and was at all times prepared, with entire self-possession and dignity, to indulge in blood-letting, to administer purgatives, prescribe hot baths, and recommend tonics. A pint of blood to reduce the pulse, then ten grains of calomel, followed in the morning by half a teacup of castor-oil containing three or four drops of turpentine to impart additional potency to the dose, and finally snake-root tea to brace up the halting system, constituted the practice in vogue in cases of ordinary fever. If this vigorous treatment failed of the desired effect, a repetition was generally resolved upon; and so the patient, sometimes enfeebled to such a degree that he no longer afforded attractive food for disease, slowly recovered in spite of this San Grado regimen. As a supplement to his professional labors as a physician, Daddy Jack indulged, in a rude way, in the art of dentistry. He understood how to cut around an aching tooth with the same lancet which he employed in blood-letting from the arm. He knew how to annihilate an exposed and throbbing nerve with a ten-penny nail heated red-hot. With the use of an old-fashioned extractor, with which to pry out an offending molar tooth, sometimes even at the expense of a fractured jaw, he was familiar. In the absence of a suitable instrument, a strong twine string, well waxed, sufficed to pull out an incisor.

On one occasion a strolling Yankee dentist visited the neighborhood. For the first time Jack beheld sundry appliances which modern ingenuity had devised for the facile extraction of teeth. In his old methods he at once lost confidence. Application was made to his master for the immediate purchase of certain designated lancets, and for pairs of forceps, both straight and curved. His wish was gratified, and the plantation was notified that he now possessed instruments with which teeth might be extracted readily and with the least amount of pain. An era of increased practice and of enlarged professional emolument quickly dawned. It really appeared as if there was scarcely a negro upon the plantation who did not have at least one tooth which "hot um," and which "eh wan Buh Jack fuh pull out fuh um." The old man's services were frequently called into requisition, and his reputation so increased that numbers from adjacent plantations sought and obtained relief at his hands.

One bright spring morning, a stalwart young carpenter, John by name, who had been suffering from a decayed jaw-tooth of huge proportions, presented himself with swollen face and most lugubrious countenance. The customary fee of a quarter of a dollar was paid in advance, and Daddy Jack made ready for the operation. Seating John in a wooden chair in the yard, and with his face turned to the sun so that the old man could "git er fair sight at de teet," Jack proceeded with his lancet to separate the tooth, as far as practicable, from the engorged and circumjacent gum. John squirmed and indulged in heart-rending groans. As the cutting proceeded and the blood trickled from the corners of John's mouth, Jack encouraged his demoralized patient with the injunction: "Tan ter um luk er man, me son. Eh yen gwine hot you much. Eh yen gwine tek long. Me mose done. Me soon git um out."

This preliminary operation concluded, Jack produced his forceps. John, already appalled at the suffering which he had endured, gazed upon the instrument with eyes

as big as saucers, and resolutely closed his
mouth. To Jack's command that he open
it, he responded: "De teet yent duh hot me
no mo. I gwine." After much persuasion
Jack prevailed upon him to open his mouth
and let him "tek de ting out." At length
the old man firmly grasped the tooth with
the forceps, and began to haul away at it.
As he pulled, John commenced to rise from
his seat. Jack endeavored, with the left
hand, to keep him down, while he tugged
lustily at the tooth with his right. All to
no purpose. John was quickly upon his
feet, and then upon tiptoe, so that Jack
could no longer operate to any advantage.
It seemed as if for once the sable dentist
was to be baffled in his aim. Nothing
daunted, however, and muttering impreca-
tions upon his unfortunate victim, he slowly
backed across the yard, drawing John after
him,—who meanwhile was giving utterance
to the most miserable and unearthly sounds
from his bloody jaws, and attempting, with
uplifted hands, to arrest the traction of the
resolute old man, who refused for an instant
to relax his hold,—until he reached a flight
of steps which led up to the main room of
the smoke-house. Here he hoped to acquire

the advantage which he so much desired. Ascending backward three of the steps, and quickly placing his right foot upon John's shoulder, so as to keep him below and thus obtain an additional purchase, with one supreme effort he succeeded in compassing his purpose. The tooth came out so suddenly that the old man, losing his balance, fell heavily against the door of the smoke-house, while John tumbled in the opposite direction, yelling with pain, and protesting that "Uncle Jack done broke eh jaw."

Recovering himself in a trice, and holding aloft the forceps, which still infolded in its remorseless fangs the gory molar, with an indescribable air of commingled dignity, scorn, and triumph addressing the discomfited victim of his professional skill, old Jack exclaimed: "Haw, Boy! when I graff my han on er teet, eh bown fuh come, er de jaw pop,—one er tarruh."

In after years the old man often recurred with manifest pride and satisfaction to this incident, and frequently cited this exploit in confirmation of his boast "dat no nigger teet ebber yet did git de better er me."

LIX.

THE NEGRO AND THE ALLIGATOR.

Foremost among the reptiles which excited the curiosity and aroused the fears of the Georgia colonists, upon their first acquaintance with them, were the alligators. Francis Moore, keeper of the stores, describing them in 1736, says: "They are terrible to look at, stretching open an horrible large mouth big enough to swallow a Man, with Rows of dreadful large sharp Teeth, and Feet like Draggons, armed with great Claws, and a long Tail which they throw about with great Strength, and which seems their best Weapon, for their Claws are feebly set on, and the Stiffness of their Necks hinders them from turning nimbly to bite." In order to dissipate the general terror which these strange saurians inspired, Mr. Oglethorpe, having wounded and caught one of them, caused it to be carried to Savannah, where he "made the boys bait it with sticks, and finally pelt and beat it to death."

To the European, newly landed on these shores, the alligator was indeed a novelty, repulsive and provocative of dread. Not so with the negro. His ancestors were well acquainted with the African crocodile, and their descendants, dwelling in this marsh region filled with swamps and cypress ponds, and permeated with lagoons, creeks, and rivers—the habitat of this formidable reptile—were from childhood familiar with its roar, and entirely accustomed to its unsightly appearance and habits. Among these sable myth-makers it figured as an important *dramatis persona*. Of the dogs, geese, ducks, and hogs of the plantation hands it was an avowed and a voracious enemy. When skinned and thoroughly boiled, its tail was esteemed by many as a savory article of food. For the cure of rheumatism its oil was held in special repute, and the exuded musk was collected for medicinal uses. Its skin, rudely tanned, entered largely into the composition of home-made pouches and shoes. Whistles and powder-charges were fabricated from the tusks, which also served a good turn for the pickaninnies to rub their swollen gums against, and to cut their first teeth upon. A constant depredator was the alligator upon the fish-traps which guarded the mouths of the short creeks emptying into the rivers. Upon the reflux of the tide, entering the inclosure, this reptile gorged itself upon the fishes there detained, and incurred the wrath of Cuffee, whose frying-pan was thus cheated out of its anticipated evening broil. Hence it came to pass that the alligator was regarded by the negro both as an enemy and as desirable game. During the spring and summer they frequently met, and whenever the former could be taken at a disadvantage its life was forfeit to the opportunity. It was killed in rice-field ditches, in shallow ponds, and occasionally upon land. The hoe, the axe, a fence rail, and the club were the offensive weapons; and loud were the cries and great was the fun while the struggling reptile was being beaten to death. In the back-waters and in swamps where the alligators made their nests, reared their young, and dug their holes, the negroes, during their leisure hours, were fond of capturing them by means of a heavy iron hook fastened to the end of a long, stout pole. This was thrust into the hole where the reptile lay. While snapping at the hook, with its irritating prong, the alligator was in the end securely caught with the barb, and then came the tug of war. It was in no wise an easy operation to draw from its hiding-place one of these reluctant, excited, and revolving monsters. For this purpose the combined strength of several stalwart men barely sufficed. The frolic was joyous, and the exultant shouts of those engaged in the sport awakened strange echoes in the depths of the dank and moss-clad swamps.

If we may credit the text of the "Brevis Narratio" of Le Moyne de Morgues, the Florida Indians were addicted to similar sport, and Plate XXVI may well be claimed in practical illustration of the amusement to which we are now alluding.

During the period of hibernation the negroes often dug these reptiles out of their holes. Sometimes the alligator attained huge proportions, measuring, from the tip of the nose to the end of the tail, fourteen feet. It was fond of a given locality, and exercised exclusive dominion over some favorite bend in the river, some chosen part of a lake, or some attractive pool in the swamp. The patriarch, with its attendant consort and progeny, there reigned supreme, unless, after severe battle, it was driven away by one more powerful.

164

In ante-bellum days, when firearms were denied to the negro population, alligators were far more numerous than they are at present. The great demand for their skins which has arisen of late, the use of the rifle in the hands of the tourist, and the employment of the shot-gun by the freedmen have united in causing a frightful mortality among these reptiles. Bartram says that when he visited the River St. John the alligators at one point "were in such incredible numbers, and so close together from shore to shore, that it would have been easy to have walked across on their heads, had the animals been harmless."

For the capture of animals drinking at the water's edge, or swimming in lake or river, the tail was employed. A stunning blow having thus been delivered, the victim was caught in the open jaws, and thence transported to the dwelling-place of the reptile, where it was guarded until decomposition had fairly supervened. It was then eaten at leisure and with apparent relish. Sometimes days were allowed to elapse before the slain animal or bird became suitably seasoned for the feast.

While hogs, dogs, calves, sheep, geese, and ducks were often captured by alligators, they seldom attacked human beings. Of mankind they apparently entertained an inborn fear, and would quit the part of the river or lagoon in which men or even boys were swimming. Instances are rare in which human life has been sacrificed to the voracity of these monsters. The writer remembers several occasions, however, on which men and children were attacked by alligators. He will be pardoned for recalling one of them.

Sawney had a wife who resided upon a neighboring plantation. It was his habit to visit his wife every Saturday night, and remain with her until Monday morning. On these journeys he would carry a bag containing provisions and such choice morsels as he had been able, during the week, to accumulate for his better half. Near the negro quarter, where he resided on the home-plantation, was a small creek, in which the tide ebbed and flowed. A large log furnished convenient means for crossing it. On the night in question, shortly after dark, Sawney shouldered his well-filled bag and set out for his wife's house. The tide was flowing into the creek. Instead of crossing on the log, he saw fit to descend the gentle bank and wade through the water. It was not more than half-leg deep, and the creek was only some ten yards wide. When he was in the middle of the stream his attention was attracted by a movement in the water. Instead of getting out upon the bank, which he could readily have done, he paused, and began to parley with what, in the darkness, he conceived to be a "sperit." "Tan back, Mossa Sperit, an lemme pass. Tan back, Mossa Sperit; me do you no harm." In this idiotic and frightened manner he stood idly talking, until what proved to be a large alligator approached and laid violent hold of his right leg. He was quickly thrown down by the reptile. In the confusion which ensued, and amid the struggles and yells of the negro, the alligator for the moment relaxed its hold, and was attracted by the fallen bag, which it tore in pieces. Sawney had so completely lost his wits, was so terrified, and was suffering so much pain, that he neglected to improve the opportunity thus afforded, and betake himself to flight. He remained rooted to the spot, howling, praying, and calling for help. Having in a little while disposed of the bag, the alligator renewed its attack upon the frightened negro, threw him down, broke his left arm, and frightfully lacerated it and one of his legs.

The negroes at the quarter hard by, hearing the noise and cries for help, armed with torches, hoes, axes, and billets, rushed to the spot just in time to save the life of the unfortunate man. The alligator was beaten to death. It measured nearly eleven feet, and was very stout. Sawney's wounds proved well-nigh fatal. He was confined to his cabin for quite three months, and, during that time, required and received the careful attention of a competent surgeon.

The lazy way in which the negro was in the habit of fishing, perched upon a tussock, with feet and rod trailing in the water, somnolent and in utter silence, did sometimes invite and receive a flirt from the tail of the reigning alligator, defending its preserves against all poachers.

The old memories are fast drifting away into the shadows, and the modern negro and the alligator of the present are but partial types of things that were.

LX

SPERITS.

Among the negroes of the coast region of
Georgia and the Carolinas a belief in the
existence of ghosts, "sperits," and super-
human influences was very general. Especially did it obtain among the ordinary field-
hands and those least educated. Compara-
tively few there were who could lift themselves entirely above the superstitious fears
born in Africa and perpetuated by tradition
in their new home. Memories of Fetichism,
of Totemism, and of Anthropomorphism
were strangely mingled with the teachings
of Christianity, and in their religious exer-
cises the emotional predominated over the
intellectual. The potency of charms and
philters was freely admitted, and it was
necessary to restrain the practice of Fetichism by positive inhibition, or by labored
persuasion of its utter absurdity. The fab-
rication of Fetiches, and their sale to those
who desired to utilize the powers of the
deities which they were supposed to repre-
sent, were monopolized by old women, who
derived considerable gain from this calling.
The idea was by such means to conjure the

neighbor against whom enmity was cherished, and thus subject him or her to the malign influences of the spirit or demon whose power was supposed to inhere in the evil charm.

The ordinary Fetich consisted of a bunch of rusty nails, bits of red flannel, and pieces of brier-root tied together with a cotton string. A toad's foot, a snake's tooth, a rabbit's tail, or a snail's shell was sometimes added. In price it varied from twenty-five cents to a dollar. To insure the efficacy of the desired spell, it was necessary that the charm should be secretly deposited under the pillow of the party to be affected, placed upon the post of a gate through which he would pass, or buried beneath the doorsteps of his cabin. Once persuaded of the fact that he had been thus conjured, the patient became possessed of superstitious fears, and often complained of bodily "miseries," which apparently defied the power of the healing art, and were wholly dissipated only when some atonement was made for the alleged wrong, or payment offered to have the spell broken through the intervention of the conjurer who had devised it.

In the conduct of plantations, difficulty and annoyance were not infrequently experienced from the interference of these old negro women,—conjurers,—who, in plying their secret trade, gave rise to disturbances and promoted strife and disquietude.

To the apprehension of the common field-hand there was no gainsaying the fact that the spirits of the departed walked the earth and revisited the scenes of their former occupancy. It was not accorded to every one to see and to commune with them. Only those "born with a caul" were capable of doing so. Such were never terrified by these ghostly visitors. By their fellows they were held in special esteem. To this favored class did July belong. I inquired, on one occasion, whether he believed in ghosts and could see spirits. "Yes, Mossa," was his reply, "me kin shum. You know me bin born wid caul. People wuh no bin born wid caul kin yeddy sperit, but dem cant shum. Sperit kin skade um, too, but dem cant skade me. Me kin walk long um der road, talk ter um een de bush, see dem een me bed, and yeddy um een de grabe yad. Me an sperit good fren."

How do they look? "Same luk wen dem bin libe, ceptin dem look lucker shadder, an dem walk backwuds, an dem face tun backwud, an de heel teh eh foot day way eh toe orter be. Dem dont tetch de groun wid dem foot, but dem sorter dis skim pon topper de grass. Dem so light dem cant mek track."

What garments do they wear? "Same cloze wuh dem bury een. Way dem gwine git any mo? De cloze hab eh shape, but you kin see dey yent nuttne eenside er um."

What do they do? "Nuttne, so fur es me know, cept walk bout, wisit dem ole home, an notus wuh duh gwine on sence dem leff."

Do they ever trouble anybody? "No, me nebber see dem trubble nobody. Dem wunt talk ter you. Dem go een gang ob two er tree, an wander bout tel sich an sich er time, wen dem haffer go back ter dem grabe. Me see dem wuk dem mouf same luk dem bin er talk ter one anurrer, an shake dem head, an pint dem finger. Dem onderstan one anurrer. Me bin question dem mo na once, but dem nebber will mek answer. Heap er time me jine compny wid dem der big road, an try fuh gage dem een conbersation, an fine out who dem yis, an how dey mek out; but dem nebber will tell me, an, befo long, look luk dem git bex, an den dey fade way een de wood an leff me lone een de road."

Can you recognize them? "Yes, Mossa, ef I bin know dem befo dey dead, I kin know dem now. Me kin see dem dist es plain es me kin see you now. Only tarruh night me bin comin from Barnedo plantation. Dest es I cross de causeway an rise de hill by Shannul ole buryin-groun me see Miley,—wuh bin dead de year arter freedom,—duh lean genst one oak tree sider de road. Day dis biggin fuh broke. Me gone up ter um an me try fuh pass de time er day wid um, fuh me yent bin see um sence dat rainy ebenin wen we bury um in Shannul. Miley look say eh bin want fuh ax me someting; an den, all ob a sutten, eh check isself, an eh tun roun an mek off fuh de grabe-yad. Me foller um, an wen eh come teh eh own grabe eh pit eh head down, an eh gie two er tree whul, an down eh gone. Me walk up en sarche de grabe. Me cant fine out how Miley git een. De grass yent mash. De groun yent broke; no hole day: an yet me see um, wid me own yeye, gone down, head foremose, een eh grabe.

"Las winter me en George bin er hunt possum een Jerrido bottom. We bin ketch two fat possum, an dest befo we mek up we mine fuh go back home we buil one fire fuh wam weself. De night berry cole. Wen we bin er wam we han an we foot roun de fire, yuh come ole Uncle Andrew, wuh nusen ter dribe fur ole Mossa, an ole Uncle Jupter, wuh bin de gadner, an ole Aunt Peggy. Dem walk up tarrur side de fire an look at we, but dem yent bin crack eh teet ter we. Me see dem plain, en me try fuh pint dem out to George. Him couldnt shum, cause George yent bin born wid caul. De dog nebber notus um. Bimeby George hair biggin fuh rise. George skade, an we leff fuh de nigger house.

"You member Jacob wuh dem bin heng een de Boro? Well, me an Sam meet um one moon-shiny night een de big road, wid de een er de rope tie roun eh neck. Me kin tell you bout heap er people me bin meet an see arter dem done dead an bury. Me shum mose ebry night. Me kin show you some ter-night ef you bin born wid caul. Many time dem people wuh cant see sperit come pon top dem an dunno nuttne bout um. Enty wen you duh walk long de road der night you suttenly feel hot win bresh by

174

you cheek? Enty you sometime smell dead man finger? Enty you yeddy bush crack der wood wen de win yent der blow? Dem duh sperit, but you no know. Sperit der walk close by you, but you no shum. Me could pint dem out an tell you who dem yiz."

Are you not afraid of these spirits? "No, Mossa; wuh me gwine fade um fuh? Dem nuttne cept de shape er people wid de sperit eenside. De bone an meat done leff um. Dem cant hot nobody. Eh breff cant pizen you; an ef eh did knock at you, eh dis same es ef win try fuh hit you."

Why do they come out of their graves? "Me dunno, cept dem want fuh see one anurrer, an wisit dem ole home, an look pon topper dem ole fren."

Are they all grown? "No, sir; you see dem all size, leetle an big, man an ooman, gal an boy, an leely baby. My leely Sue, wuh dead, blan come an play bout de house ebry now an den. One time me try fuh ketch um up in me arm, but me han gone clean tru um dis luk er shadder, an den eh wanish, an me so sorry."

These notions of July may be accepted as typifying the belief on this subject entertained by the great majority of the negroes on the coast. Many went a step further, and invested these ghosts and "sperits" with the ability to intervene in mundane affairs, and to entail harm and misfortune upon those with whom they had not lived amicably while in the flesh. It was the belief of some of the African tribes that the power of a ghost bore some relation to that which the being possessed when alive, and it may be that an inherited thought affords at least a partial explanation of the ideas still entertained by their descendants upon the shores of this New World.

XLI.

DADDY JUPITER'S VISION.

Dreams are intimately associated with the lower forms of religion. . . . During sleep the spirit seems to desert the body; and as in dreams we visit other localities and even other worlds, living as it were a separate and different life, the two phenomena are not unnaturally regarded as the complements of one another.—SIR JOHN LUBBOCK.

Daddy Jupiter was an old man when I first knew him. In the capacity of a body servant he had accompanied his master during the campaign of 1812-15; and this fact, apart from his excellent character, elevated him in the esteem of all. For many years prior to his death he was practically "off duty," keeping in-doors whenever he did not feel entirely well, and in pleasant weather working in the vegetable garden. He was fond of his chickens and pigs, and cultivated on his own account a small patch where arrowroot, long collards, sugar-cane, tanniers, ground-nuts, benne, gourds, and watermelons grew in commingled luxuriance. A widower and without children, he led, in the main, a retired life; seldom visiting at the houses of the other negroes on the plantation, but always chatting pleasantly with all who came to see him. At the "Praise-House" his seat was never vacant

when his health permitted him to be present,
and he filled the office of a "watchman"
upon the plantation. It was the duty of
one occupying that station to advise in spiritual matters, to lead in the semi-weekly
prayer-meetings, to set an example which
others might well follow, and to counsel in
all religious difficulties. Although some-
what quick-tempered, and jealous of that
respect which he deemed his due from
others, he was upright, honest, full of Christian sentiment, and pronounced in his con-
demnation of everything savoring of evil.
In a word, he was a man of good reputation,
enjoyed the confidence of his fellows, stood
high in his church, and was supposed to be
in special favor with the Lord.

During the winter preceding his death
Jupiter suffered much from rheumatism.
For weeks together he ventured no further
than the door of his cabin, where he would
sit and sun himself and smoke his clay pipe.
A negro lad, Cæsar by name, had been
deputed to cook for him, to wait upon him,
and to minister to his needs.

I called one morning to see the old man,
to inquire after his health, and to ascertain
whether his wants were properly supplied.

For an hour and more he entertained me, as was his wont, with tales of the olden time, and was evidently in excellent spirits. As I was about to depart, Cæsar said: "Mossa, Uncle Jupiter bin hab er wision las night. Leh him tell you bout um." My curiosity being excited, I resumed my seat, and inquired: "Daddy, is that true? Have you had a vision?" "Yes, me chile," he answered, "me suttenly did hab er wision, an er berry good one too." "Tell me about it," I rejoined. "Well, yeddy me," replied the old man, and he spoke as follows:—

"Las night, dis befo fus fowl crow, me bin er leddown een me bed. De moon done set. Cæsar, him bin ter sleep by de fire een de tarruh room. Eberyting on de plantation gone bed. Me bin study bout de time wen ole Jupiter hab ter meet him Lord and Master, an me berry happy een me bussum. Den me drap ter sleep. How long me bin ter sleep me dunno, but all ob er sutten pear like ebry shingle an boad hab er crack, an de light stream tru, an de room bin bright es day. Wile me duh wonder wudduh dat, four leely angel, wuh dress een wite an hab wing on eh back, fly een de room. Two light topper de foot er de bed, an one on

179

arur side er me. My! but dem bin pooty!
Me see heap er pooty wite chillun een me
time, but me nebber bin see nuttne teh come
up ter dem, nur ter ketch nigh um. Dem
look pon topper me so kind, an dey open an
shet dem wing, an mek sich a cool breeze een
de house. Bimeby me retch out me han fuh
tell de one huddy wuh bin tan close me bed
on de right side, but eh draw back, an eh
say: 'Jupter, we come fuh leh you know
de blessed Jesus duh commin fuh cahr you
up ter Hebben an show you de seat wuh eh
hab ready fur you.' Me dat glad me yent
hab bref fuh mek ansur. Me hard fuh
bleebe me own yez. Me harte rise up een
me troat, an me yent duh say nuttne, but
me duh watch fur de Lord. Soon de blessed
Jesus, wid de print er de nail een eh han
an eh foot, an wid de star on eh head,
drap right down tru de top er de house dout
crack er shingle, an eh call me name, an eh
tell me fuh rise, an eh pit eh han onder me
shoulder, an eh liff me up light es er fedder.
Me ole cloze an me ole body leff behine, an
somehow narruh me sperit, him keep de
shape er de body. Den eh pit eh han onder
me arm, an eh cahr me way up eenter de element, beyant de sun an de moon an de star,

an de leely angel duh foller we. We gone an we gone way up tel we git ter er big alablaster house, wid high piazza all roun an roun, wuh shine same luk de sun, buil in de middle er a beautiful gaden wid flower, an fruit, an hummin-bud, an butterfly, an angel wid harp duh sing an duh joy ehself onder de tree. Dis es we git ter de big gate, wuh mek wid pearl, eh swing open dout tetch um, an de blessed Jesus lead dis poor ole nigger up de shinin pate to de big house way de Lord lib.

"We gone up de step an enter de pahler, way de great God bin er set on eh golden trone. Den de blessed Jesus mek de good Lord sensible dat dis duh Jupter wuh him hab sabe, an dat eh fetch um fuh show um eh seat wuh eh done prepare fur um. Wid dat de Lord, him call teh one angel, an eh tell um fuh bring one chair an set um down befo eh trone. Soon es dis bin done eh say: 'Jupter, yuh you chair; set een um. Eh blants ter you.' Mossa, you nebber bin see sech chair een all you life. Eh hab gold rocker ter um. Eh hab welwit cushin een eh bottom. Eh hab high back, an eh arm stuff. Eh so soffe an easy. Eh look pootier den dat big rockin chair wuh ole Mossa bin gib Missy wen eh marry you farruh. Me shame fuh set een de chair, but de blessed Jesus, him courage me, an me tek me seat, an me so tankful dat me hab one chair een de mansion een de sky.

"Den de blessed Jesus tell anurruh angel fuh bring me some milk an honey fuh drink. Eh bring um een a nice glass tumbler, an eh gen me fuh drink. Me tase um, an eh sweet mone anyting me ebber drink een me life. Eh tell me fuh drink um down, an wen me drink all outer de glass, an me yeye ketch sight er de bottom er de tumbler, me see some speck. De ting trouble me, fuh me dunno wuh mek speck day een de bottom er dat clean tumbler. Den de blessed Master notus me, an eh say: 'Dont fret, Jupter; dem speck duh you sin, but now dem all leff behine.'

"All dis time me bin er set wid me face tun way from de Lord an eh trone, cause eh so great an bright me couldnt look pon topper um. Mossa, me cant scribe wuh me see an yeddy een dat Hebben. Eh yent fuh tell. De blessed Jesus tek me tru de gaden, down by de ribber, an een de orchud way de bigges peach, an fig, an orange, an pomegranate, an watermillion, an all kin der fruit der grow. Me see heap er good people wuh me bin know befo eh dead. Ole Mossa, Cappne Maxwell, ole Mr. Ashmore, Buh Jack, Sister Masha, me own Dinah, an mo bin day, an dem all hab harp, an bin der sing, an walk bout, an der pledjur ehself. Dem glad fuh see me too, an gen me de right han er fellership.

"Arter me bin in Hebben good wile, de blessed Master, him say: 'Come, Jupter, I gwine show you way de bad people go.' Den eh lead me down to one bottom wuh dark an kibber wid cloud. In de fur een me see smoke duh rise, an me yeddy people duh cry an duh holler so bad. Wen we git ter dat spot, lo an behole! day was de mouf er Hell. Satan, him bin day wid eh pitchfork, an eh black head wid screech-owl yez, an eh red yeye, an eh claw-han, an eh forky tail. Eh tan right at de mouf er de big hole way de smoke an de fire duh bile out. Fas as de tarruh debble bring sinner ter um, eh push um wid eh pitchfork an eh trow um een de fire. Lord Amighty! Mossa, how dem sinner did kick an holler an try fuh pull way! But twant no use. De minnit ole Satan graff eh claw on um eh gone, an you could yeddy um duh fry een de fire same luk fat

183

een me pan yuh. Me bin rale skade. De ting mek me sick. Me hole on ter me Jesus, an him tell me not teh fade, dat nuttne shill trouble me.

"Dis at dat time me wake. Me hair bin a rise on me head, an wen me come fuh fine out me bin een me own bed, an fowl bin a crow fuh day. Oh, Mossa! dat ting wuh dem call Hell duh a bad place. Me no wan shum no mo, an me yent gwine day nurrer. Enty de blessed Jesus done show me de chair wuh eh done sabe fuh me een Hebben? Yes, Mossa, me seat eh fix, an ole Jupter ready fur go wenebber de Lord call."

He was indeed prepared, and early in the spring we laid him to rest beneath the venerable live-oaks which, with their solemn arms, guarded the plantation burying-ground. Then, not in a vision, but in reality, as we believe, the good old man claimed and was accorded his seat in the "mansion not made with hands, eternal in the Heavens."

GLOSSARY

Abnue, avenue
Agg, egg
All ob er sutten, quickly and unexpectedly
An, and
Arter, after
Arur, each, either
Ax, ask

Bactize, baptize
Bague, to beg
Barruh, barrow
Beber, beaver
Bedout, without
Ben, bend, bent, been
Berry, very
Bes, best
Bex, vex, vexed
Bidness, business
Biggin, begin, began
Bimeby, by and by, presently
Binner, was, were
Bittle, victuals
Blan, in the habit of, accustomed to
Blanks
Blants } belongs to
Bleebe, believe
Bleege, obliged, compelled
Bodder, to bother
Bode, board, boards
Bofe, both

Bole, bold
Boun, resolved upon, forced to
Bredder, brother
Bref, breath
Bres, breast
Bresh, brush-wood, to brush
Broke up, to leave, to depart
Brukwus, breakfast
Buckra, white man
Bud, bird
Budduh
Buh } brother
Buhhine, behind
Bun, burn
Buss, burst, or break through

Cahr, carry
Caze, because
Ceive, deceive
Cept, accept, accepted, except
Chillun, children
Chimbly, chimney
Chune, tune
Cist, insist
Clorte, cloth
Cloze, clothes
Cohoot, bargain, agreement
Cole, cold

Conjunct, agree to, conclude

Cote, court

Crack eh teet, make answer

Crap, crop

Crape, scrape

Cratch, scratch

Cut down, disappointed, chagrined

Darter, daughter

Day, there, is, to be, am

Day day, to be there

Den, then

Der, was, were, into

Dest
Dist } just, only

Destant, distant, distance

Det, death

Diffunce, difference

Disher, this

Do, door

Dout, without

Drap, drop, dropped

Duh, was, were

Dunno, don't know

Dut, dirt

Edder, other

Eeben, even

Een, in, end

Eenwite, invite

Ef, if

Eh, he, she, it, his, her, its

Element, the sky, upper air

En, end

Enty, are you not, are they not, do you not, do they not, is it not

Faber, favor

Faid, to be afraid

Fambly, family

Fanner, a shallow basket

Farruh
Farrur } father

Feber, fever

Fedder, feather, feathers

Fiel, field

Fine, supply with food, find

Flaber, flavor

Flo, floor

Flut, flirt

Foce, force

Forrud, forehead

Fren, friend

Fros, frost

Fuh, for

Fuh sutten, for a certainty

Fuss, first

Gage, engage, hire

Gedder, gather, collect

186

Gelt, to girt
Gem, to give
Gen, gave, again
Gie, give
Gimme, give me
Glec, neglect
Glub, gloves
Gooly, good
Graff, grab
Gree, agree, consent
Grine salt, fly round and round
Guine ⎫
Gwine ⎬ going, going to

Haffer, have to, had to
Hair rise, badly frightened
Haky ⎫
Harky ⎬ hearken to, heed
Han, hand
Hanker, long for, desire
Hatchich, hatchet
Head, get the better of
Head um, get ahead of him
Hebby, heavy
Holler, halloo, hollow
Hoona, you
Hot, to hurt
Huccum, how happens it, why, how come
Huddy, how d'ye do

Ile me bade, grease my mouth
Isself, himself, herself, itself, themselves

Jew, dew
Jist, just
Juk, jerk

Ketch, catch, reach to, approach
Kibber, cover
Kine, kind
Knowledge, acknowledge, admit

Labuh, labor
Lass, to suffice for, to last
Lean fuh, set out for
Led-down, lay down
Leek, to lick with the tongue
Leely ⎫
Leetle ⎬ little
Leff, to leave, did leave, left
Leggo, to let go
Leh, let
Lemme, let me
Lenk, length
Libbin, living
Lick, to whip, stroke of the whip
Lickin, whipping

187

Lick back, turn rapidly back
Lief, leave, permission
Light on, to mount
Light out, to start off
Long, with, from
Lub, love
Luk
Lucker } like

Mange, mane
Medjuh, measure
Mek, make, made
Mek fuh, to go to
Mek out, fare, thrive, succeed
Member, to remind
Men eh pace, increase his speed
Mine, mind, heed, take care of
Miration, wonder, astonishment
Mo, more
Moober, moreover
Mona
Moner } more than
Mona dat, more than that
Mose, almost
Mossa, master
Mouf
Mout } mouth
Murrer, mother

Mussne, must not
Muster, must have

Nabor, neighbor
Narruh, another
Nebber, never
Nekked, naked
Nes, nest
New Nigger, a negro fresh from Africa
Nigh, to draw near to
Notus, notice, observe
Noung, young
Nudder, another
Nuff, enough
Nummine, never mind
Nurrer, neither, another
Nuse, use, employ
Nussen, used to, accustomed to
Nuss, nurse
Nuttne, nothing

Obersheer, overseer
Offer, off of
Ole, old
Ooman, woman, women
Out, to go out, to extinguish
Outer, out of

Pahler, parlor
Passon, parson
Pate, path
Pen pon, depend upon

188

Perwision, provisions
Pinder, ground-nuts, pea-nuts
Pint, direct, directed, point
Pintment, appointment
Pit, put, apply
Playpossum, to fool, to practice deceit
Pledjuh, pleasure
Po, poor, pour
Pon, upon
Pooty, pretty
Pose, post
Prommus, promise
Pruppus, on purpose
Pusson, person

Quaintun, acquainted with
Quaintance, acquaint-ances
Quile, to coil, coiled
Quire, to inquire, in-quired

Rale, very truly, really
Range, reins
Rastle, to wrestle
Retch, to reach, to arrive at
Ribber, river
Riz, rose
Roose, roost

Sabe, to know
San, sand
Sarbis, service, kindness
Satify ⎫ satisfied, hap-
Saterfy ⎬ py, content
Scace, scarce
Schway, to swear, swore
Scuse, excuse
Seaznin, seasoning
Sebbn, seven
Sed, sit, sat
Sed-down, sit down, sat down
Shet, shut
Sho, sure
Sholy, surely
Shum, to see it, see him, see her, see them
Sider, on the side of
Sisso, say so
Skade, scared
Smate, smart
Sofe, soft
Soon man, very smart, wide-awake man
Sorter, sort of, after a fashion
Sparruh, sparrow
Spec, expect
Spose, expose
Spute, contest the cham-pionship with
State, start, begin
Steader ⎫
Stidder ⎬ instead of

Straighten fur, run rapidly for
Stroy, destroy
Sukkle, circle, fly around
Summuch, so much
Sutten, certain, sudden
Suttenly, certainly, suddenly
Swade, persuade
Swode, sword

Tack, to attack
Tackle, to hold to account
Tan, to stand
Tarrify, to terrify, to annoy
Tarruh }
Turruh } the other
Tase, to taste, taste
Tay, stay
Tek, take
Tek wid um, pleased with him, her, or it
Tek you foot, to walk
Tel, until
Ten, attend to
Tend, intend
Tenk }
Tenky } to thank, thanks
Ter }
Teh } to
Tetch, touch
Tetter, potatoes
Tick, thick, abundant, a stick

Ticket, thicket
Tickler, particular
Tief, to steal, thief
Ting, thing
Tird, third
Titter, sister
Togerruh, together
Tole, told
Topper, on top of, on
Tote, carry
Trabble, travel
Tru, through
Truss, trust
Trute, truth
Tuff, tuft
Tuk, took
Tun, turn, return
Tun flour, to cook hominy

Up ter de notch, in the best style
Usen, to be in the habit of

Vise, to advise
Vive, revive

Wan, to want, to wish, want
Warse, wasp
Wase, waste
Way, where
Wayebber, wherever

Whalin ob er, enormous, severe
Wid, with
Wile, while
Win, wind
Wine, vine
Wish de time er day, to say good-bye, how d'ye do
Wud, word
Wudduh dat, what is that
Wuffer, what for, why, what to
Wuh, what, which, who
Wuhebbuh, whatever
Wuk, work
Wul, world
Wunt, will not, would not

Wurrum, worms
Wus, worse
Wus den nebber, worse than ever
Wut, worth

Yad, yard
Yearin, hearing
Yeddy, to hear, to hearken to
Yender ⎫ not, was not,
Yent ⎭ were not
Yent day day, is not there, are not there
Yeye, eye, eyes
Yez, ear, ears
Yiz, am, is, to be, did
Yuh, here

Zamine, examine

NUMBERS

One, one
Two, two
Tree, three
Fo, four
Fibe, five
Six, six
Sebbn, seven
Eight, eight
Nine, nine
Ten, ten
Lebbn, eleven
Twelbe, twelve
Tirteen, thirteen
Foteen, fourteen
Fifteen, fifteen

Sixteen, sixteen
Sebbnteen, seventeen
Eighteen, eighteen
Nineteen, nineteen
Twenty, twenty
Tirty, thirty
Forty, forty
Fifty, fifty
Sixty, sixty
Sebbnty, seventy
Eighty, eighty
Ninety, ninety
One hundud, one hundred
One tousan, one thousand

191

MONTHS OF THE YEAR

Jinnywerry, January
Febbywerry, February
Mache, March
Aprul, April
May, May
June, June

Jully, July
Augus, August
Sectember, September
October, October
Nowember, November
December, December

DAYS OF THE WEEK

Mundy, Monday
Chuseday, Tuesday
Wensday, Wednesday
Tursday, Thursday

Friday, **Friday**
Sattyday, Saturday
Sunday, Sunday